Out to Pasture

Out to Pasture

(but not over the hill)

Effie Leland Wilder

with illustrations by Laurie Allen Klein

Guideposts®

CARMEL • NEW YORK 10512

This Guideposts edition is published by special arrangement with PEACHTREE PUBLISHERS, LTD.

Text © 1995 by Effie Leland Wilder
Illustrations © 1996 by Laurie Allen Klein

Jacket illustration by Laurie Allen Klein
Book design by Loraine M. Balcsik
Book Design by Terri Fox
Composition by Composition Technologies, Inc.

Manufactured in the United States of America

Library of Congress Cataloging-in-Publication Data

Wilder, Effie Leland
        Out to pasture / by Effie Leland Wilder.
            p.cm.
        ISBN 1-56145-101-0
        I. Title.
    PS3573.I4228O93   1995   94-48008
    813′ .54-dc2O   CIP

To the dear memory of
Frank
who kept me laughing

All the people who inhabit these pages
are products of my imagination, except for
Arthur Priest, who resembles a living person.
That person has freely given me his permission
to use the character.
—*ELW*

Acknowledgments

I would like to give heartfelt thanks:

To Cada McCoy, owner of All Books & Company of Summerville, who "god-mothered" this book;

To Bruce Covey and the other nice people at Peachtree Publishers, for picking my manuscript out of the pile, and for treating me with much kindness;

To Bessie Mell Lane (who could have posed for Retta, herein) who was unfailing in her encouragement, as were my children and my friends here at the Presbyterian Home and elsewhere;

To Marian Lord, my Peachtree editor, who worked with me patiently in polishing the manuscript;

To Laurie Klein for her attractive illustrations;

And to each nice person who has put out good money for a very small volume by an unknown author. I *do* hope you will be rewarded.

—ELW

Contents

1

FairAcres

December 1st

I simply can't resist any longer. When Augusta—or Gusta, as we all call her—described why she wanted her funeral luncheon catered, I knew I just had to start putting down some jottings about life here at "The Home." They won't be jottings, really; typing will be easier on my hands.

I've set up my faithful old Royal, and I'll keep a loose-leaf notebook. I will work on this right after *Jeopardy* and before the nine o'clock movie. I wish I had started this practice the night I got to FairAcres, fourteen months ago, and had caught my very first impressions. Anyway, here goes.

Gusta is one of my tablemates. Eight of us are assigned to each table in the dining room for a period of two months. Then it's fruit-basket-turnover time. I will hate to part with a few of my mealtime companions next week, but not all. I won't much mind saying bye-bye to Augusta Barton.

She can be entertaining at times, but she talks a mile a minute, nonstop. What with bragging and eating and complaining, her mouth gets a continuous workout. Much of her complaining is about her daughter-in-law Inez. Inez is why Gusta wants a caterer to handle the luncheon after her burial.

"I've written out my Final Instructions to my son," she announced. "Which preacher, what hymns, which clothes, which pallbearers—everything. And I want my funeral collation to be catered!"

"You want your *what* to be *what?*" somebody asked.

"I'm going to make all the arrangements for the food and entertainment after the burial. I don't want Inez making her Low Country Tuna Casserole or her Potted Meat Paté. Those things are so bad they'd make my friends sorry they paid me the respect of coming. If Inez has to cook, she'll get tired and flustered, which will take away part of her pleasure at getting rid of me."

Some of us raised our eyebrows at that. Gusta insisted, "Of course she'll be glad to get rid of me! I guess she's pretty good as daughters-in-law go, but I'm sure that in her mind I'm a Problem with a capital P. And everybody's glad when a problem goes away, no matter in what direction!"

Gusta noticed that her ice cream was melting, so she tackled it and we had a few quiet seconds to digest the thoughts of arranging a catered funeral luncheon and of writing out "Final Instructions."

I haven't written any. Maybe I should. I know I don't want any eulogies or any emotional hymns to make people cry. Sometimes in the vast commixture of Gusta's babbling there's a smidgen of substance.

December 3rd

Tonight after supper I went into the library to look at a copy of one of the good magazines The Home subscribes to. I sat on the sofa near the door to the brick terrace where some folks like to sit in good weather. It had been a very mild day, and, of course, the heating system continued to operate at its December level. Two men were sitting on the terrace, and I enjoyed the fresh air from the door they had left slightly ajar. As it turned out, I inadvertently also enjoyed their conversation. They were talking about a plane that was flying over our bailiwick, low and loud.

"Sometimes I wonder if those fly-boys know how high our long-leaf pines are. Gonna clip 'em one day," said Curtis. "Paul," he asked his companion, "have you ever been up in a plane?"

"A few times," came the answer. "Have you?"

"Once. Just once. I didn't want to, but my Mama was over in Georgia visiting relatives, and she got real sick. They phoned me and said I'd better get there quick. So the only thing to do was to fly to Atlanta, so I did—but I'll tell you something, Paul…"

"Yeah, what's that?"

"I never did put my whole weight down!"

They thigh-slapped over that remark for at least five minutes. Then they started comparing notes on Geneva Tinken, a highly vocal resident here.

"I'm scared of that woman, Paul," said Curtis. "Spreadin' tales is her favorite indoor sport."

"I know," said Paul, "she's sitting at my table. She's dangerous. Last night I couldn't sleep, and I made up some lines about her. Want to hear 'em?"

"You know I do."

"O.K.—

Mistress Tinken
I'm a-thinkin'
You're a stinkin'
Old coot!"

Curtis laughed 'til he choked, and I had to leave the library for fear they would hear me chuckling.

One way I can use this journal is to respond to a letter from my college classmate Henrietta Gooding telling me that she has put her name on the waiting list for this home, and telling me of her great misgivings. She asked me to write to her in detail about FairAcres Home.

"Give it to me straight," she said. "I haven't put any money down, and I can get my name off the list, or get it put on the bottom. God knows there wouldn't be time for it to rise to the top again!"

I am inserting a copy of my letter to her. (Every day I

think of something I sold or gave away that I wish I had, but thank goodness I kept my slightly beat-up portable typewriter.)

Dear Retta,

I loved your letter. I know what you mean about decisions, about uncertainty, about your name moving up the list for this place. I agree that waiting around for people to die is "ghoulish." When they phoned me and said my name had reached the top of the list (had crept up via trips to the cemetery, I knew), it hit me like a blow. I wanted to sit down and bawl.

Even though life had become right much of a briar patch, and even though I had made the application and gone through all the motions, I suddenly found I wasn't ready for the smooth grass of pastureland. Not yet. Maybe next year. Maybe in five years. But I knew that if I waited too long, they might not take me. You have to be able to dress yourself, and walk to the dining room.

Getting here wasn't easy. Closing up a house where I had lived for forty-seven years was the worst trauma I have ever experienced. Memories of Sam and the children hit me with every drawer and closet I cleaned out. The attic nearly did me in.

I finally had to start pitching, and I felt like I was throwing my life away and my family's lives. You know what killed me? Leaving the door to the den! On the back of that door were measurements of our children through the years. Sam would put a ruler on the child's head, make a mark with the name by it, and then show each child how much he or she had grown since the last birthday. They were so proud of those marks, and now I'm sure they are painted over. Oh, me.

I survived, however, and I'm here, and now I'm mostly glad. Not altogether, but mostly. At least the children know that I'm safe (there are security guards and an infirmary with nurses) and that they won't have to figure out how to make room for Mama. They would have done it, and with good grace. But would I have had the necessary grace? And would a grandchild who lost a room have hated it?

You said it would help if I put down some of my impressions and sent them to you. I had been thinking about starting a diary, or even a story ("The Last Chapter," maybe?), but I have been lazy about it. So now I am glad to be spurred on by your request. I will try to write something down nearly every night, and you can read these jottings when you come to see me to "case the joint."

Meantime, please keep writing to me. Your letters will help keep the dust out of my mailbox. It's a much bigger box than I need for my hot correspondence with AARP, Ed McMahon, and

Medicare.

Not only that, but I enjoy your style. Your wit and fluent pen take me back to meetings of the Wild Thyme Literary Society at Converse College. Remember what scared freshmen we were at our first meeting, when they had us read something we'd written?

The funniest thing was the name of that group. I remember when a girl got up in the dining room and said, "There will be a meeting of the Wild Thyme Society in the library tonight." I pricked up my ears—Wild Time? Oh, boy! But in the *library?*

I stray, as usual…There are a lot of really nice people here. They take some discovering, because they're quieter than The Nuts. I will probably be spending most of my writing time on The Nuts. They're much easier to portray.

I enclose copies of my first "jottings," which will not convey much of an idea of this "Home, Sweet Home." But more will come, *deo volente.*

Much love,
Hattie

December 7th

One really good thing about this place is that we are all members of the same generation. When people talk about

Ronald Colman or Billy Sunday or Lum 'n Abner or Lydia Pinkham or Studebakers, they don't have to stop and explain.

I heard a lady the other day ask, "Tom Cruise? Who's he?" When told he was one of the hottest movie stars around, she said, "Shoot. I'm a Joel McCrea fan myself." I made a circle with my thumb and finger to show her I agreed. Old Joel was a love. He looked and talked and acted like a man.

Perhaps we can't work computers and are a little embarrassed because our youngest grandchildren can. But, on the other hand, there are some of us who can write sonnets. We have one woman here who makes up crossword puzzles and has sold several of them to *The New York Times*. People in our conversational French class are parlez-vooing all over the place.

Many of us can knit handsome sweaters and can crochet heirloom items with intricate, beautiful patterns. One resident makes all of her clothes from scratch, starting on a loom! She lives in one of the cottages and has turned her second bedroom into a "loom room." She weaves the yarn into the softest materials, which she fashions into stylish skirts and dresses. That takes patience, and more care and work than most young people want to invest these days, it seems to me.

Some of us in our tiny kitchens turn out some wonderful things: artichoke relish and orange marmalade and blueberry preserves, among other things. So you see, everything is not rocking-chair and Medicare.

Not only do we have the same kinds of memories; many of us seem older than we are because we absorbed our parents' memories. Children in the old days sat quietly at the table under threat of punishment, and there was nothing to do but listen to visiting aunts and uncles and grandparents as they held forth—sometimes interminably.

When my cousin Boo Starrett came to visit, it was kind of fun. I didn't squirm as much listening to her because I was waiting for her to get things mixed up. Mama told me when I was about twelve that Cousin Boo's mix-ups were called malapropisms. I was proud to learn such a long word. Cousin Boo would say things like, "My friend Tooty has a hyena hernia. They're bad." And when she was trying to get a driver's license she said she had to learn "paralyze parking."

One day she said, "I told him if he did that, it would be catamount to throwing in the towel."

I thought of Cousin Boo the other day when I heard one of the residents here say, "The dogwood trees didn't look right this year. They must have a plight." That was the same lady who said, after hearing someone complain about a meal, "Well, I'll tell you something. That dinner tasted real good to me. Of course, I'm no common sewer." And the rest of us—not a connoisseur in the crowd—had to try to keep straight faces.

I may not get too many words tangled, but I find I've been getting an embarrassing number of details mixed up recently, such as the days of the week, the days of the month, the day for putting out the garbage, the day for the dentist, the day for paying my monthly maintenance fee, the day for making a deposit *before* writing the checks!

From what I hear, I'm not alone. I've decided that the main religion in this place is not Presbyterianism. It's Confusion-ism. We are the Mother Church, and I am an elder.

December 8th

Louly's door was slightly ajar, and as I passed down the hall I heard what I thought was crying. I pushed the door a bit, and sure enough, Louly was in her chair by the window, bent over and weeping.

"It's Hattie," I called. "May I come in?"

She gave me a come-on motion with her hand. I shut the door and went over to her.

"What is it, Louly?" I asked, holding on to her shoulder.

She shuddered, and then said in a shaking voice, "I... don't...want...to...get...any...older!" Then she bent over again and shook with misery. "I hate it...I despise it—everything about it. And it gets worse every day...I thought things might get better when I retired and came here, but no. Just aches and pains. There's nothing to look forward to but a new ache in a new place." The last two words were a wail, and the tears started again.

I patted her shoulder, wondering what to say. She blew her nose, straightened up a little, and continued.

"When you've worked hard and tried hard, it looks like

your life should get better toward the end, not worse." The sadness on her face as she looked out of the window was painful to see. "Lucius said today at lunch that his life would really be pitiful if it wasn't for his memories. Well, Hattie, I'll tell you something: I haven't got good memories. My life is pitiful and always has been...How could it have been anything else with a face like this?"

She looked up at me. Tears softened the faded eyes, but nothing softened the shape of the nose, or the unfortunate mouth.

I started to speak, but no words came. I couldn't make myself say, "Oh, your face is all right, Louly." It wasn't all right. It was pitiful—a darn shame—a loathsome trick to have played upon you.

"I used to run home from school," she went on, sniffing and blowing, "racing to show Mama my report card. She'd say 'That's good, Louly.' But she didn't really care. I could tell. You should've heard the way she carried on when Theresa came home and announced she'd been made Junior May Queen, or Miss Ninth Grade."

"Was Theresa your sister?" I asked. She nodded. I reflected, as I had many times, on the cruelty of a plain girl having a beautiful sister. What could I say to this poor creature?

I patted her shoulder again and said, haltingly, "I'll bet you were a wonderful teacher, Louly. I'll bet you inspired many a youngster—left your mark on them for life."

"Humph. Some mark. A fifth grader's memory of an ugly woman who could be mean because she was unhappy." She looked out at the trees, her mouth drawn down. "I'll tell you something, Hattie. Don't ever tell anybody; but I had the audacity to love a man once, a principal at the school where I taught. He was nice to me, out of the goodness of his great heart, and I leaped at that goodness and tried to make something more out of it...All I got was disappointment and embarrassment."

I thought of some lines by Dorothy Parker:

> "The sun's gone dim, and / the moon's turned black;
> For I loved him and / he didn't love back."

I didn't say them out loud, of course, and she melted into sobs of self-pity again, saying something that sounded like, "What's the good of any of it?"

I squeezed her hand and said I would see her a little later, and I slipped out, feeling as helpless and depressed as I had ever felt in my life. What's the good of it, indeed, with a life like that? But I know that I have to find a way to help that miserable woman. Now that I think about it, I don't believe it's the thought of further aging and death that gets her down, as much as it is the fact that she hasn't done much living—good living, that is.

December 9th

I walked around the perimeter of our campus late yesterday afternoon. When I passed the Lyerlys' cottage, I noticed Arthur Priest washing and polishing the Lyerlys' car. Arthur is one hardworking young man. Nearly every

day and on Saturdays, he does overtime jobs for the
residents to supplement the salary he makes in our maintenance department, and he does the jobs superbly. There is
nothing that he can't clean or paint or put back together.
Whatever he mends stays mended.

I was so impressed with Arthur when I first came—at
the way he could hang pictures and arrange furniture and
put up curtains—that I asked Cora Hunter how FairAcres
could afford to keep such a fellow. "He ought to be using
those talented hands in manufacturing or inventing or even
decorating," I said.

"Oh, but he can't," said Cora. "I mean he could, but he
can't get to those places to do those things. He can't drive."

"Can't drive!"

"He's not allowed to drive," she explained. "He doesn't
have a license."

"No driver's license? Why ever not?" I was incredulous.

"He's tried several times to get one, but he can't read well
enough to figure out the test questions."

"Didn't he go to school?" I asked.

"Yes, but there must be something wrong. He couldn't
pass the tests, and finally when he was about fifteen he
quit and went to work. He got married at nineteen," Cora
continued, "and had two kids right away. The family lives
in a tiny trailer about a mile from here, so he can ride his
bicycle to work, which is lucky for us."

Indeed it is, not only because of his amazing efficiency,
but also because of his very likable personality. Arthur

knows all of us, smiles and calls us by name whenever he runs into us, and seems genuinely interested in our welfare. What a difference that kind of positive attitude makes in a staff member.

Later that night I was still thinking about Arthur—his dark good looks, his nice nature, and the trap he was caught in. Surely somebody could teach him to read. I never studied that reading method—what is it called? Lorback? I never taught school, but surely, among the two hundred people here.... And then it hit me! Louly! I wanted to jump up and go see her right then, but it was after eleven, so I waited until this morning. I wasn't disappointed.

"Arthur? That nice young man who fixed my commode? You mean to tell me he can't read?" A gleam came into Louly's eyes. "Why, Hattie, do you really think I might help him?"

"I believe you could do a better job of it than anybody else in this whole place. You spent many a year teaching children to read, didn't you?"

"That I did. And a few of them were a real challenge, I can tell you. Some were just lazy and no-account—but I had two that had dyslexia."

"That's what I think is Arthur's trouble. Do you know how to handle that?"

"If that's what it is," said Louly, "then he's not seeing the words right. It takes patience and time to help him—more time than public school teachers have—but what else have I

"Sometimes we spend fifteen minutes figuring out one word..."

got to do? I'd love to work with that boy. Anybody who can be that polite and nice while he's fixing a commode is worth helping."

December 15th

I think it's working! Arthur jumped at the chance to get help. It is usually evening before they can get together, what with Arthur's after-hour chores. They meet in the library, which is a pleasant room and usually deserted at night.

Louly had saved some of her textbooks, which they started on, and she called the state library for assistance. She must have gotten the right person, because they have already sent her some books on dyslexia and told her where to order some special reading manuals. She has also gotten much help from that wonderful group, the Literacy Association.

Yesterday, Louly told me, "Sometimes we spend fifteen minutes figuring out one word, but he is so smart he immediately relates it to a whole class of words."

As she talked, Louly beamed. I wish I could say that she was suddenly pretty. She wasn't, but she looked glad to be alive and that made her much easier to look at.

December 16th

One of the residents who is nearly blind came into the chapel for the service this morning, late. As she turned into a row about midway down, the rest of us held our breaths.

We could see what she couldn't: that there was not an empty seat on that row.

We had visions of the sedate lady squatting into a gentleman's lap. It would have been a dreadful embarrassment to her and to him. Fortunately a kind soul stood up and led her back into the aisle and found her a seat. Disaster was averted. There's kindness here, all around. I see it more and more.

The staff arranged for two doctors to come and have a session with us about how to improve our memories. I thought, Oh, boy! That's for me! The only trouble was, I forgot to go! I hope my children don't hear about that.

Cora told me a "funny" tonight. Maybe it's an oldie, but it was new to me. An old lady said to the bartender at a party, "Just put a jigger of water in the glass and fill it up with whiskey." When the bartender looked astonished, she lowered her voice and said, "You see, I can hold my liquor, but I can't hold my water!" Whoo-eee.

Last night I heard a comedian on television say, "I had a Christmas card from my paper boy. It said 'second notice.'" He said when the paper boy came to collect, he told him, "You'll find your money in an envelope up in that tree— right where you usually throw the paper."

2

Sarah

December 17th

Sarah Moorer sits at the table next to mine in the main dining room. I had noticed her pleasant expression and shy smile in passing, but I had had no contact with her until we met one day this fall in the library. I'm on the Library Committee and was on duty that day.

I could tell she wasn't finding what she wanted as she browsed through the shelves, and I offered to help.

"You don't have enough books by Conrad Richter," she said. "I've read all of these, most of them twice."

"So have I!" I was glad to find someone who shared my enthusiasm for *The Trees, The Fields,* and *The Town.* We agreed that those three books form an unsurpassed trilogy.

"They should be required reading in every eleventh grade

in the country," said Sarah.

"You're so right. History classes, or English?"

"American history, I suppose, although they're magnificent literature. He has caught the Early American pioneer idiom to perfection. He never really had the acclaim he deserves."

I heartily agreed. Conrad Richter had been a favorite of mine for years, and yet it seemed that few people even knew his name. I decided I liked this bright-eyed lady. She appeared to be about seventy—young for The Home.

During the fall, I went to see her in her room on D Hall, and she came to my apartment in the new wing for tea and conversation several times. I could tell that she liked to get out of that "institutional" main building, although she never disparaged her neighbors on the hall where she lived.

I knew that she had one sibling, a brother, and was grieved when someone told me at lunch today that he had died and that Sarah was leaving that afternoon for Atlanta to arrange his funeral.

I cut my lunch short and went to her room. Her suitcase was on the bed ready to close. She sat facing the window. As I tapped on the open door and came in, she turned toward me with a look that hurt my heart.

"Hattie, he was my first playmate." I hugged her. The frailness of her body added to the hurt. "He was so good to me."

"Was he older or younger?" I asked.

"Three years older. He felt he had to look out for me, and

he did it so sweetly. No little girl ever had such a brother. He used to straighten my sash and my hair ribbon when we started out for Sunday School, and made sure my socks matched. He cared more about how I looked than my mother did. But he was not a *sissy*. He could fight with the best of them."

She sobbed a little. I patted her and found her a tissue.

"Will there be anyone in Atlanta to help you?"

She shook her head. "There're no relatives."

"Does he...did he live in an apartment house?" She nodded. "Then maybe there will be a neighbor or two..."

She nodded again. "It was a neighbor, a Mrs. Peabody, who called to tell me that they had broken into his place after getting no answer at the door or on the phone. They found him dead in his chair. Heart failure, the doctor said."

"Maybe Mrs. Peabody is a kind soul. I hope so...I wish I could go with you..."

"No, no, Hattie, I wouldn't think of it. For one thing, I can't afford to pay your way. You see, Richard helped pay my maintenance fee here." Her mouth drooped. "I don't know exactly how things are going to be from now on. I just have my teacher's pension..."

"From what you tell me, I'm sure your brother made arrangements for your care after he was gone."

"Maybe so...I know he would have, if there were any way..."

Sarah had an hour before leaving for the airport, so I stayed with her. She seemed to want to talk about Richard, so I asked her questions.

"When you moved here, why didn't your brother get a room here, too, or an apartment?"

"I was so hoping he would. He had retired from Emory University—he was a physics professor—and they continued to pay him a small salary as a consultant. So he had to stay in Atlanta."

"Was he a widower?"

"No. He never married." Her tears came again. "I was so happily married to Jim. We had such wonderful companionship. It makes me sad to think of Richard's life. He had so little joy."

"Oh, Sarah, do you *know* that?"

"Yes, Hattie, and I blame Mama. You see, Rich was only nineteen when Papa died. He was just a boy, a freshman in college, and he suddenly had three people to support. Mama didn't make any attempt to do anything but whine. She was good at that."

Her mouth quivered. "It's terrible to feel that way about a parent, but I can't help it. And I don't feel too much better about Papa. He was attractive and lovable, but improvident. He died owing everybody."

"So Richard had to take over?"

She nodded. "He left school and got two jobs. I was able to help a little, doing baby-sitting and working on Saturdays in a grocery store. Rich was determined for me to finish high school and go to college. He knew I wanted to be an English teacher."

"And you *did* go to college."

"Oh, yes, and so did he, finally. He was a whiz at physics and was able to get scholarships. But he still had to work like two dogs to take care of the three of us. It took him almost ten years to get his degrees. He was well into his thirties when he finally got the job he wanted: teaching in college. His youth was gone—and he really hadn't had any youth—or any fun. No girls...just grind, grind, grind."

She shook her head sadly at the memory and continued, "By that time Mama was a chronic invalid and had to be in a nursing home. You know what *they* cost. She lived in that home for twenty-eight years! Poor, dear Richard. And now he's gone without having had any of the...the highs of life."

She broke down again. "Oh, Hattie," she wailed, "if I could have only told him good-bye...and thanked him. I loved him so..."

December 21st

I thought about Sarah many times in the next week, wishing that there could be someone to go to Atlanta and help her. I knew that she had been happily married to a fellow teacher who had died two years ago, just before she moved here. They had had one child, a son who was killed in Vietnam; and now her beloved brother was gone. How many blows could she stand?

As soon as I heard she was back I hurried to her room. She stopped unpacking and greeted me with a warm hug.

"I hope it wasn't too hard on you, Sarah—the funeral, and everything."

"No, Hattie, it wasn't. I had to be thankful that he went so quickly, no long-drawn-out suffering.... But it was something I discovered after the funeral that has really helped me." Her eyes were actually sparkling. "It's quite a story. Do you have time to hear it?"

"Of course. But let's go to my apartment. I'll make us some tea, and I have some cheese biscuits. We'll lock the door and have a good confab."

Sarah told me about meeting Ursula Peabody, her brother's neighbor. "I don't know what I would have done without her," she said. "She met me at the airport—and it's a long way out of Atlanta. Wasn't that good of her? Then she went with me to the funeral home and helped me make the arrangements. She phoned some people who had known him, and there was a nice turnout for the service and burial—but, oh, Hattie, it was something that happened later that I want to tell you about!"

Her face beamed. I couldn't imagine what was coming.

"I had to clear out his apartment. He had lived there for years, so it was quite a job. On his desk there was a tape player with a tape in it. Out of idle curiosity I turned it on, wondering what Rich had been listening to at the last. A woman's voice came on, in the middle of a sentence. She was saying, '...so you see, I won't be able to meet you next weekend. I can't tell you how sorry I am—but there will be other times.

"I cut the tape off and sat there stunned. I knew that voice, or I had known that voice at some long-ago time. Who in the world?...I turned the tape on again. She thanked him for reading to her, on a recent tape, Ben Jonson's 'Song to Celia.' She said she had heard it sung many times, but 'to have it read to *me*—just to *me*—in *your* voice, was a heart-stopper.' She begged him to send another tape soon, and then she said, 'Tell you what. Let's set our clocks and think about each other at eight o'clock on Friday night. Tell you what. Let's do it at eight on Saturday night, too, and on Sunday night.'

"Hattie, I recognized who it was who used to say 'tell you what' all the time, just like that. It was Serena Horner."

Sarah's eyes shone as she told me about Serena, a girl two years older than Sarah, that she and Richard had grown up with.

"Somehow I had forgotten that Richard had been interested in her—more interested than any of us knew, apparently. I remembered their having a few dates, and my plaguing the life out of him by trying to listen in on their phone calls. I remembered their going to the junior-senior prom together. But after Rich started working two jobs, there was no dating time."

Though she had lost touch with Serena and her family when the Horners moved away from Greenville, South Carolina, Sarah explained that she remembered Serena's best friend, Betsy Kane.

"And I did know Betsy's married name and whereabouts,

so after two phone calls, Serena and I were talking to each other for the first time in decades. Ah, but Hattie, I had to tell her that Richard was gone. I heard her gasp, and I felt so helpless; but after a minute she said she was all right and asked if he had suffered.

"I was glad to tell her that the doctor said death was instantaneous. She said that she had been fearful because she hadn't heard from him in several days. I told her that I would like to see her, and the next day I took a bus to Athens and spent six hours with Serena.

"Hattie, she turned out to be lovelier than she had been as a girl—and she was such a pretty girl. Betsy had told me that Serena's husband, who had been a professor, was now an invalid, confined to bed, and *non compos mentis*. Utterly. No mind left at all. There was Serena, trapped with him, with no children to help her, and not much money."

Sarah described how Serena and Richard had met again when he went to a seminar in Athens and called his old flame.

"Serena told me that he had been her first love, and she had never forgotten him—and that it was the same with him. Rich told her that even after he became financially able to get married, he couldn't, because he was tied to her memory. So, he kept coming back to Athens, sitting with her in the living room of her apartment, with poor, invalid Jamie in the next room coughing and wheezing and babbling, making the strange noises that I could hear as she and I talked."

"Poor Richard," I couldn't help saying.

"Yes, Hattie. It was a sad setting for a renewed romance.
I walked arm-in-arm with Sarah back to her room. We
were both filled with strong emotions as she continued
with the story of her visit. "Serena said, 'It isn't as if we
upset Jamie, or did him any harm.'"

Sarah smiled, "And oh, let me show you something I
found in his top desk drawer. He had written these poems
out, to send her I'm sure. She has them now. This is a copy.
For a man who was a scientist, and not very literary, I think
he made some good choices, don't you?"

I agreed after reading these excerpts, which he had put
down in his strong, masculine hand (so much better than
typing them).

"'For thy sweet love remembered
    such wealth brings
That then I scorn to change my state
    with kings.'—Shakespeare, Sonnet 29

"'No spring nor summer beauty
    hath such grace
As I have seen in one
    autumnal face.'—John Donne
"(It's not *that* autumnal. Much of spring remains.
    R.M.)

"'If equal affection cannot be
Let the more loving one be me.'—W. H. Auden

"(Don't be troubled over these lines, my dear. I agree with them, but I really believe, in our case, they are unnecessary. R.M.)

"'As easy might I from myself depart
As from my soul, which in thy breast doth lie;
That is my home of love. If I have ranged,
Like him that travels, I return again.'
                                    —Shakespeare, Sonnet 109"

I left Sarah's room and walked back to my own place, hoping I wouldn't meet anyone who might say, "Going to supper?" or "Cold enough for you?" and shatter my strange mood, which lay somewhere between heartbroken tearfulness and a lovely exaltation.

That's what romance can do to a woman at *any* age.

December 24th

Tonight I played the piano for the Christmas Eve service in our chapel. At the end, someone turned out the lights, and by candlelight we softly sang "Silent Night." It was beautiful.

Then we went to the small dining room for punch and cake. Somebody suggested we sing "Happy Birthday, Dear Jesus," which we did, but that didn't please me. Somehow, I felt a little impertinent serenading the Master with that hackneyed tune. It's not exactly, but *kind* of like saying to the Queen of England, "Have a nice day, Queen." Maybe I'm being picky, but it seems to me there should be a different birthday carol for Him—not the everyday one that is used for every Tom, Dick, and Harriet.

I saw Gusta earlier today when I went through the lobby going for my mail. She was sitting reading the morning paper. So as not to just walk by without speaking, I said, "Anything good in the paper today?"

"I don't know," she said. "I just look at it to see the weather, and who's dead."

Not even Christmas seems to improve her spirit.

December 27th

Ellen Caine is a lighthearted soul. She can make a joke out of almost anything. Laughter emanates from any table in the dining room where she sits.

Today she had on a sweatshirt that her son had given her for Christmas. The message printed on the front read: "You know you're getting old when the Happy Hour is a nap!"

Blessings on Ellen Caine and her bright temperament. We need her in this place. But with Ellen it has to be a one-on-one situation, or a very small group. She has been asked numerous times to share her wit from a platform at our talent shows, but she declines. She says, "If anybody lines me up to talk from a stage, I'll call in dead!"

Ellen regaled us one day at lunch, telling about a woman

of fine family in her hometown who managed to combine Southern ladylike-ness with some of the instincts of a drill sergeant. Mrs. Perry was the woman's name, and she drove an old, old black Packard that had a special dignity about it.

One day Mrs. Perry went to Charleston to shop, cruising down narrow, one-way King Street at about five miles an hour as usual so that she could enjoy looking in the store windows. On this particular occasion she saw a stunning dress in Kerrison's display. When she slowed down even more to get a good look, her old car died on her.

She fiddled with everything on and under the dashboard, but nothing happened. Finally the annoyed man in the car behind her began to blow his horn. Mrs. Perry got out of her car, Ellen reported, went up to the man's window, and said to him very sweetly, "Young man, if you will go up there and start my car for me, I will stay here and blow your horn for you."

And Ellen said he did it!

3

Angela

January 7th

A new resident named Angela Pryor moved into one of the larger apartments last week, with much *Sturm und Drang*. The hallway of G-wing has hardly been passable because of the tools of all the activity inside. She's repapering, repainting, raising counters to a new height (Mrs. Pryor is statuesque), and—someone said—replacing FairAcres' nice little chandelier with a Tiffany model.

There has been much talk at meals about "La Pryor" and her Cadillac and her diamonds and designer clothes. Cora Hunter, who moved here last year from Columbia, told us that Angela is the widow of a man who had been president of South Carolina's largest bank, headquartered in Columbia.

"After Mr. Pryor died," said Cora, "it nearly killed her to give up the job of 'Mrs. President.' To make up, she started running the garden club, the D.A.R., and even her church—including the Session, the Women, *and* the choir! I'm sure she thinks they'll all fall apart now."

Cora is a mild little lady. Her vehemence about Angela surprised me, but after I had a few encounters with the person in question I understood Cora's attitude. It soon occurred to me that "Mrs. President" had it in mind to become the C.E.O. of FairAcres Home.

Her first assault was on the kitchen. She complained of nearly every meal. The poached eggs were as hard as rocks, the bacon too greasy, the coffee too weak, and the vegetables much too overcooked.

"I always thought corned beef hash was just for the help," she pronounced. "And do we really have to have chicken four times in a row? How about some lamb? Or some fresh salmon?"

"Dream on, friend!" someone sang out.

January 21st

Angela hates the business of sitting at table with the same people for two months. After two weeks at Table Six, she asked Mr. Detwiler to move her; but since she could come up with no reason except boredom, he refused—much to the sorrow of the Table Six-ers. They were more tired of her "airs and graces" than she was of what she probably considered their bucolic mindsets.

So the lady was not exactly Queen of the May at FairAcres Home, and her popularity took a further plunge this week when she stormed into the administrator's office—and later into the dining room—saying that Arthur Priest had stolen an heirloom brooch from her room where he'd been working the day before.

There was a shock wave of dissent. "Arthur? Arthur Priest? The very idea! He wouldn't filch a straight pin, much less an heirloom!"

"Well, I know he did!" insisted La Pryor. "My new living room draperies finally came yesterday, and Arthur put them up. And now my pin is gone. It was my grandmother's wedding gift from my grandfather: diamonds and sapphires in the shape of a crescent. It was *per*-fectly *beau*-tiful. Oh, I could just die. I'll get that young thief if I have to—"

Somebody broke in and asked, "Were you in the apartment with him the whole time?"

"No. I went downstairs to get my mail. So you see, he had ample time to go into the bedroom and raid my jewelry chest. I just *know* he did it. Why don't they put him in jail?"

I'm told that when she reported the matter to the office, one of the staff said, "Mrs. Pryor, no one else on your floor has reported any thefts." Angela replied, "Humph! They don't have anything worth stealing."

After making a search of Mrs. Pryor's room himself, Mr. Detwiler had been forced to call in the local police. An officer came out and, after a long questioning of the suspect, reported that he did not believe Arthur had stolen the brooch.

The administrator and the policeman questioned all the service staff, anyone who had access to that floor of the building; but to no avail.

Someone saw Arthur going back to the maintenance department after the questioning and said he looked pale and upset. We were afraid he might give up his job. No doubt he wanted to, but the thought of supporting his family would come first with him.

So that's how matters stand; and I, for one, wish that a certain creature had found a retirement home nearer to her borough in the Up Country.

January 22nd

Louly Canfield and I decided we would go to see Arthur at his home this afternoon after work. We wanted to let him know that most of us believe him innocent. We drove in Louly's car. She knew the way to his trailer, which is on a side road about a mile away.

It was a warm day for January, and Arthur's wife, Dollie, was in the yard playing with two adorable little boys. There was a picket fence and a slide and sandbox, all made by Arthur I'm sure, and all surrounded by carefully tended grass and shrubbery.

Dollie was surprised to see us, but she asked us in, very politely. She latched the gate behind us, leaving the children to play where she could watch them from inside, and led us into her neat little home.

"Little" is the operative word. I know trailers are

compact, but, oh dear! I can't imagine how four people manage to exist in this one's dimensions. I'm not sure, but I think there is only one bedroom.

Dollie insisted on making us some tea. The miniature kitchen was open to the living room, so we could talk to her while she worked. Pretty and sweet-faced, she was a pleasure to watch. She told us that her mother lived in Drayton and came out each weekday morning to drive Dollie to work and keep the boys. It seems that Dollie herself works four hours a day helping at the high school lunchroom.

"Aren't you lucky that your mother lives close by?" one of us said.

"Oh, yes! I don't know what in the world we would do if it wasn't for her," she said as she brought us cups of tea with lemon and homemade cookies. "Miss Canfield, I've been wanting to meet you and thank you for teaching Arthur. He's been like a different person since the lessons started. He had some hope. Everything was getting better—until yesterday."

"We know about yesterday," I said. "That's why we're here."

"I see Arthur coming home now on his bike," said Dollie, who was standing near the window. "He was one put-out person last night. He wanted to go back to North Carolina to his father's tobacco farm, but I think I talked him out of that. They just barely scratch a living there, and there wouldn't be anybody to help him learn to read."

We could hear the boys outside joyfully shouting "Daddy! Daddy!" Arthur played with them a few minutes and then came inside.

"Miz McNair, Miss Canfield, good evenin'. I thought I recognized Miss Canfield's car out there."

There was dark stubble on his cheeks and chin. It was the first time I had ever seen him not neat and shaven. It make him look younger, somehow, and more vulnerable.

"Arthur, we just came to tell you how sorry we are—how sorry so many of us are—about Mrs. Pryor's accusations," I said. "We know they are not true."

"No, ma'am, they're not. I've tried to be real good to everybody at that place. Some of the ladies remind me of my grandmother—but not *that* lady."

We talked a little about how he might defend himself. Louly asked him what time he left the Pryor apartment.

"As soon as I got the last curtain hung. It must've been about noon because I went right out to that bench by the pond and ate my lunch. Dollie fixes me a bag lunch every day."

"Was anybody else eating there?"

"No, ma'am."

"Did you see anybody in the hall when you came out of the apartment?"

"No, ma'am. I could hear through the doors that some of the folks had their TVs on."

"Well, I'll tell you what, Arthur," said Louly, "you hang in there. We're not going to let you take the rap for something you didn't do. You've got a lot of people on your side...I hope you'll meet me tomorrow night for your lesson."

"No, Miss Canfield. I think we'll have to let the lessons go for now. I'm just too upset. I hear that lady has contacted the Home's head office in Charlotte, and they're sendin' someone down..."

"Surely they wouldn't do that...over just a lost brooch," I said.

"Well, it seems Miz Pryor has some pull. Her husband was a big shot...Excuse me, please." He got up and went into the bedroom. Dollie's eyes followed him, full of misery.

We made our good-byes to her and to the solemn children peeping through the screen door. They had come up to the top step, sensing something amiss.

Going home Louly drove too fast. "I'm so mad I could *spit!*" she said, bringing her palms down hard on the steering wheel. "That nice little family! Hattie, I'm going to get to the bottom of this theft if it's the last thing I do."

"That makes two of us...Louly, have you ever seen Angela Pryor wearing that pin?"

"No, and neither has anybody else that I've talked to. She could've made the pin up, for all I know."

"Well, I think she owns the pin, and I think it's still in her apartment. I'll tell you why."

I told Louly that the night before, I had recalled something from my childhood. My mother had lost her engagement pin—breast pins, they called them in those days. She turned the house upside down, with no results. Weeks later, when she had given up on finding the pin, she found it in the very back of her closet, pinned to the lapel of a suit she seldom wore.

"My mother was wonderful, but she was not a very organized person. Maybe Angela is not either."

"Mr. Detwiler says he and the housekeeper helped Angela look through her apartment."

"O.K. But I think you and I could do a better job of looking. And we've got a good motive!"

"Hmmmm," Louly nodded. "How can we possibly get permission?"

January 30th

We didn't get permission. In fact, we couldn't do anything for two days because Angela Pryor was in her room, confined with a slight cold. The grapevine reported that she had heard from the home office, and they were sending someone down the next week to investigate.

On Thursday, Louly and I paid a visit to Fred Boling, the head of maintenance. He assured us that he was on Arthur's side.

"That boy wouldn't take nobody's pin," he said. "I'd swear to that."

We told him that there was a chance of Arthur's losing his job, with no recommendation for another one. He agreed to help us in any way he could. When we told him that we needed a key to Mrs. Pryor's apartment, however, he looked dubious.

"Fred," I said, looking him right in the eye, "you know that Miss Canfield and I will do nothing in that place but hunt for that brooch."

"Yes'm, I know that...O.K., I'll get you a key. For goodness sake, don't ever let a livin' soul know I did it."

We promised, and dashed to Louly's room, with the key in my hand, to make our plans. We decided that we needed a confederate, but we wouldn't tell her where we got the key.

We settled on Cora Hunter. We knew she was trustworthy, and were pretty sure she'd have the gumption to help us. Sure enough, she agreed without a second thought.

"What we want you to do, Cora, is to invite Angela to the Sunday afternoon concert."

"What concert is that?"

"The string quartet from the Charleston Symphony is coming here to play in the Methodist Church. We'll get you two tickets. All you have to do is persuade Angela to go with you."

"I think I can do that," said Cora. And she did.

Angela came back to the dining room on Saturday, recovered from her cold, and seemed pleased at Cora's invitation. (She had received few invitations from the residents, especially lately.)

On Sunday, as soon as we knew the two ladies had taken off for the church, Louly and I went to work. We slipped into the

Pryor apartment at a time when the residents were napping, sleeping off the effects of too much Sunday dinner.

Believe it or not, I closed my eyes for a few seconds and asked the Lord to bless our search; not to forgive our sin, but to give us a diamond and sapphire pin. "We need it, Lord, *so bad*."

We locked the door behind us and started on the dressing table and chest, removing drawers and contents carefully. Then I headed for the large closet. I took each dress and suit out separately, searching every inch of each one, in case the pin had fallen and was caught in a fold or pocket. Then I put the garments on the bed in the right order for putting back. The bed was soon piled high. My, the woman had a wardrobe!

If I hadn't been so furious with her, I might have admired her taste. As it was, all I could think was that Arthur and Dollie could live for weeks on what she had spent on two or three of those outfits.

I held up a gorgeous "opera suit." The skirt was of lilac silk, the blouse of lilac crepe de chine, and there was a flowered chiffon jacket in deeper shades of lilac.

"My goodness, Louly, where do you think she expected to wear *this?*"

"Oh," replied Louly, turning around to look, "she came to the reception for new residents in that. Showing off, of course!"

Suddenly my hand hit something sharp, caught in the folds of the flowing chiffon collar. It was the brooch!

It was a matter of breaking and entering.

"Louly!" I exclaimed. "Louly, look!"

It *was* a beautiful piece of jewelry. We looked at it for a long time and then looked at each other as the same thought struck us both. *What do we do now?* All we had worried about was finding it. We had given no thought to what the finding would entail.

It was a matter of breaking and entering. We had no right to be there. We had to cover our tracks, and at the same time, we had to make sure that the pin was discovered.

"Let's think, while we're putting everything back," said Louly, very sensibly. "Oh, Hattie, I don't care what happens...I'm so glad we found it! I'd like to see her expression. Couldn't we just leave it, staring up at her on her night table, to astonish her good?"

"Heavens, no, Louly. She'd know somebody had been in here. What we've got to do now is to get everything back exactly where it was, including the pin on this dress, and then...then, I'll think of something."

I thought half the night and finally came up with an idea. I tried it out on Louly the next day, and she approved. I took the key back to Fred, thanked him, and told him he would hear some good news later. Next I called the head of the Library Committee and laid the groundwork for my plan; and then I went to Angela's apartment.

She was completely surprised to see me, but became more and more cordial as I explained the reason for my visit. I told her that some of us on the Library Committee were thinking of putting on a fashion show to make money for some new books. Plans were tentative, but if we had it, we'd like for her to model two or three of her best outfits.

"Oh, my, I'd love that!" (I had had no doubt.) "I just ordered and received a holiday dress from Nieman Marcus that is stunning. Let me show you!"

It was stunning all right: Georgette embroidered with pearls. Where on earth did she expect to wear such a thing, I thought to myself.

"That will be elegant," I said out loud. "Now we'll need two more. Someone told me you wore a lovely thing—I think it's called an opera suit—to the Newcomers' Reception. How about that?"

"Oh, yes…my lilac. How sweet of someone to have noticed. Let's find that."

She found it and laid it on the bed. The pin was covered by a layer of chiffon. *I must be careful.*

"Now, one more," I said. We decided on a navy and white cruise outfit. "Maybe we need a more everyday selection, and not both of these dressy numbers," I ventured. "Let's see which one would be best."

I held up the new holiday dress, scrutinized it, and then held up the opera suit. I managed to shake it a little, and the brooch appeared. "Oh, my! Look!"

"For heaven's sake," said Angela. "My pin!" She looked stunned. "I can't believe it. I searched this closet…"

"Of course you did." I tried to keep my voice calm. "I can easily see how you'd miss it, covered up like it was. Thank goodness the mystery is solved."

"Yes," she replied, uncertainly. It did me good to see that her conscience was gnawing at her.

"I'm sure you will want to let Mr. Detwiler know right away—and Arthur—"

"Yes...I don't suppose you would want to tell them?" Her voice was softer than I'd ever heard it.

"Why, I'll be glad to give them the good news. Perhaps you'd better phone the Charlotte office. I understand they were going to send somebody down—"

"Yes, yes. I'll call them right away. You'll let me know the details of the fashion show later?"

"I will. Two more members of the committee have to approve it, so it's not a sure thing, but I hope we can have it. Good-bye now...and congratulations on finding that heirloom!"

Angela smiled weakly, and let me out. I felt like giving what the mountaineers call "a whoop an' a holler." I wondered if she would have the grace to apologize to Arthur.

February 28th

A list of birthdays is kept in the office, and somebody noticed that Angela would have a birthday shortly. She is extremely shut-mouth about her age—clams up if there is any mention of things like the year of graduation from college, or anything that would date her. But Cora had found out, through a friend in Columbia, that Angela would be eighty on her "next."

She had become so unpopular after the Arthur incident that a plot evolved to deluge her with cards saying "Happy Eightieth!" But the plot was foiled. A few days before her natal day she took off on a Caribbean cruise. If there was any celebration of her entry into her ninth decade, it took place on the high seas.

Before she left she had been slightly subdued. I had actually begun to think that it might be barely possible to begin to like her; but when she returned, she was back to normal: entirely satisfied with herself and a trifle scornful of everybody else.

Since the residents here are largely good-natured, tolerant, friendly people with no "airs," she was a misfit. No one shed a tear when she soon decided to seek quarters in an Episcopal home in Augusta, which she said would have "a more congenial atmosphere." There were no farewell parties.

Arthur began to smile again, and so did Louly, because he asked her to start teaching him again. Life at FairAcres has returned to what it was pre-Angela. Praise the Lord.

4

Kudzu Kottage

June 2nd

There's been a considerable hiatus in my journal-keeping. In early March there was a small epidemic of flu here, and I succumbed. Soon after I got back on my feet I had a relapse and ended up feeling like "the tail end of misery."

The only good thing about it was that I learned who my friends are and that they are dear, caring people. I also learned that our nurses are super.

I didn't have the strength to go near the typewriter for weeks, and I got out of the habit of "jotting." It took too much energy. Maybe I needed Hadacol! I missed a whole spring.

But now summer is here, and life seems more desirable every day. (Some shots of B-12 have helped, I'm sure.)

Anyway, I shall try to be more faithful to my self-appointed task of chronicling events at FairAcres. Incidentally, the acres are looking fairer to me every day. The sap *does* rise, even at my great age.

June 10th

A minister came to talk to us last week. In fact, he gave a series of lectures on "How to Handle Grief."

After the first lecture, the attendance was very poor. He was a fairly young man. We could have given him a postgraduate course in handling grief.

How we hate to have people get up on a podium and talk down to us, as if we were children. As if he's saying: "You poor dear old things. I know it's hard being on your last legs. But there, there. We'll try to find something to make you smile, as you limp into the sunset."

Phooey! Double phooey! We want to hear something stimulating, something to oil up the wheels of our minds, which are still functioning, thank you.

We had another visiting minister recently who was of the "Leave 'em with a Point to Remember" variety. (I like that kind. *One* point. We can remember *one* point, possibly.) He took as his text a verse from Romans, chapter eight. He called it one of the most powerful and most cheering and comforting verses in the Bible. He ended by saying that most telephone books have a few numbers listed on a page in the front for emergencies—fire, police, ambulance.

"Everyone should write on their hearts the following,"

he said. "In case of any personal or spiritual emergency, dial Romans 8:28—'We know that all things work together for good to them that love God, to them who are called according to God's purpose.'"

June 13th

High-style skirts seem to be either droopy-long or sassy-short these days. I'm wondering how much shorter the short ones can get. Is there a point of no return?

In years to come, children will have to say, "I learned it at my mother's bare knee." Oh, dear.

I think an undue strain is being put upon pantyhose, to avoid *really* indecent exposure. Anyway, I worked two lines out of the situation:

> A clothing budget would be a cinch,
> If mini-skirts were priced by the inch!

June 16th

Some days I rush to my apartment from the dining room and grab pencil and paper so that I can quickly jot down the "overheards" in shorthand before they vanish into oblivion. My attention and retention quotients have gone down sadly in the last two or three years. I'm glad I got here in time today to record a gem from the lips of Gusta Barton. (She and I are tablemates again after several months.)

Gusta goes to her mailbox just before dinner, and as we

eat she apprises us of her Medicare situation, of her exciting communications from Ed McMahon and reminders from her dentist, and of the doings of her hometown church, which is good about sending her bulletins and newsletters.

Today she opened a letter from her son, and in a minute she dropped her spoon in outrage.

"Shoot!" she said. "Harry has sold off an acre of land behind the old home for five hundred dollars. That's no kind of a price! It was a great *big* acre!"

June 21st

I can still hardly believe it. Another "inmate" and I actually went for a walk with two men yesterday after supper. We had what might be called, in our restricted lives, a tiny adventure.

Men are in short supply here, but there are two widowers who are not only *compos mentis,* but are able to walk a few blocks with the help of only canes, not walkers. Lucius Grover and Sidney Metcalf were sitting on the patio digesting their hominy and corned beef hash when Christine Summers and I came out to get some air before the evening news programs started. (By the way, it feels like the middle of the afternoon when they feed us supper here—especially with the bright evenings of daylight savings time!)

Anyway, Lucius said, "Come on out, ladies. Sid and I were just talking 'bout takin' a little stroll to see how those Cape Jessamines are doing along the front of our penal compound. Wanna go with us?"

In our widowed and lonely states, if two men had asked us to walk with them to see a ditch full of poison ivy, Chris and I probably would have accepted gladly.

The four of us strolled to the Home's gate. We examined the gardenia bushes with their lavish and fragrant blooms and were turning around to come back when Sidney said, "There's a road going down towards those woods that I've been wanting to explore. Anybody game?"

We looked at each other and nodded in agreement.

Lucius said, "There's plenty of daylight left, so why not? Just so Geneva Tinken doesn't see us. She'd break the wheelchair speed limit, spreadin' the word that the four of us were eloping—or worse."

We had to laugh. Geneva's chief end is to make trouble and sully reputations.

FairAcres is on the outskirts of Drayton. The town's streets run out before they get to us. After going through the gate, we turned to the left and walked down a dirt road.

"Last winter when the trees had fewer leaves I caught a glimpse of a house down this way," said Sidney. "It may be just a shanty—not worth the trip—but something about it interested me, and...I don't know...I was just intrigued. I'd like to take a better look."

After a few minutes we came upon the house, set back about fifty feet from the road, behind a picket fence that had fallen into decay. We stopped and stared, unbelieving.

"I'll be dog," Lucius said. "Did you ever see anything like that?"

The house was enclosed by that "Bane of the South," kudzu vine. We could barely make out the shape of the little building under the masses of big green leaves that not only covered it, but seemed to be devouring it.

We stood still. Christine said, "I don't think I want to go any closer. It's kind of scary."

The tall trees hovering overhead deepened the shadows. It was an eerie sight. The vines covered most of the pines and had apparently crept across the yard to the steps, then the porch, then the walls and roof of the empty house, seeming to clutch it in strong green arms.

"I'm going to see if the kudzu has gotten inside," said Sidney. Lucius followed him. They stumbled through the thick greenery on the steps and porch, holding each other up. With their canes they pulled back vines that were covering a window and peeped in. Then I saw Sidney pull at a vine over his head. He got enough loose to reveal a piece of once-white gingerbread trim, just under the edge of the porch roof. We could barely make out what appeared to be three dormer windows upstairs.

I made my way gingerly to the porch and jerked at a stubborn vine. I couldn't break it, but I pulled off enough leaves to see a bit of porch railing with a fancy spindle.

We walked home slowly, filled with wonder that a quaint Victorian cottage could have been abandoned and taken over by what Chris called "the vicious tree-eating, house-eating monster."

"I'll be dog," Lucius said.
"Did you ever see anything like that?"

"I remember hearing that kudzu was imported from Japan seventy-five years ago to be used as a porch vine," Sidney said.

"That was sure smart," chuckled Lucius. "Probably someone in Washington had *that* bright idea.... I know one thing. You can practically *see* the stuff grow. I remember somebody sayin' a long time ago that kudzu and Yankees were takin' over the South. I'm beginnin' to believe it."

"Do you suppose there's anything we can do?" I asked. "I belonged to the Preservation Society at home. We worked hard to hold on to any structure that had any historic or architectural value. Kept the town from tearing down two houses. In fact, we moved them, restored them, and sold them."

"Good for you," said Sidney. "The South is waking up. I wonder who owns that house. How could we find out?"

I lay in bed last night thinking about "Kudzu Kottage." (What a sickening name. Like those tacky names on beach houses: "Bide-a-Wee" and "Dew Drop Inn.") I'm determined to track down its story.

Later

Paul and Curtis were "at it" again tonight after supper, and I, sitting near them in the window (unbeknownst), was ripe for a laugh. It had been a rough day. Sally Pugh lost her bottom teeth, and everybody on our hall turned out to help her find them. We finally took her bed apart and found them between the sheets, but by that time she was trembling and crying.

I was also depressed because of some words by that lovely young man, James Hilton, who—bless him—gave us *Lost Horizon* and *Goodbye, Mr. Chips*. I was re-reading *Lost Horizon* and came upon a discourse between the High Lama and Conway, in which the High Lama says:

> "The first quarter-century of your life was doubtless lived under the cloud of being too young for things, while the last quarter-century would normally be shadowed by the still darker cloud of being too old for them; and between these two clouds, what small and narrow sunlight illumines a human lifetime!...A slender, breathless and far too frantic interlude."

I had been ruminating about how slender and breathless those few years of my "interlude" now seemed to me; frantic at times, too—and it saddened me. So I was glad when I listened to my two "merry men" conversing, and heard Paul give a chuckle.

"What's funny?" asked Curtis.

"I was thinkin' of two fellows I heard about—Joe and Ed—eatin' breakfast in a café. Ed noticed something funny about Joe's ear. He said, 'Joe, did you know you've got a suppository in your left ear?'

" 'I have?' replied Joe. 'A suppository?' and he pulled it out and looked at it hard and said, 'Ed, I'm glad you saw this thing! Now I know where my hearin' aid is!'"

Whooo-*eee!* What would my mother have thought of that? Nothing, probably, because she wouldn't have understood it. And if by some slim chance she had understood it, she wouldn't have believed that her daughter would have dared to report the story, even to her private journal. Oh, my.

June 22nd

Lucius came to my table tonight at supper and said, "I want to see you on the patio when you've finished." I nodded, and he went on. I could feel seven pairs of eyes on me. One pair belonged to Geneva Tinken and plainly and hopefully communicated questions like, "What do we have here? A little hanky-panky?" *Oh, Lord!*

When I got to the patio the other three conspirators were already in whispered conference. (We had agreed to keep our discovery a secret for the present.) Lucius told us that he had gone to the maintenance department and engaged two of the workers to do "a special job" for him on Saturday morning. "I told them to bring ladders, wire cutters, and machetes. They're about to die of curiosity...Do you ladies want to go with us?"

"I do," I said, and looked at Chris, who nodded but said, "Won't we be trespassing? Did you find out anything, Hattie?"

I shook my head. I had told them I would call my friend Amelia Easley, a resident of Drayton, and try to find out who owned the cottage. Amelia is the daughter of my college roommate, Lucy Furman, who was born and raised in Drayton but now lives in Asheville. "Amelia and her family are at Hilton Head on vacation, and I didn't know anyone else to call... Do you think maybe we ought to talk to a lawyer?"

"Not yet," said Lucius. "We won't go inside the house." He scratched his head. "I don't see how anybody could fault us for tryin' to keep a nice little house from bein' et up."

"Right," said Sidney. "We'll just pull off the vines and that's all. It shouldn't take more than two or three hours."

June 25th

How wrong Sidney was! Obviously he had never had any close transactions with *"Kudzu karoliniana."*

The two workers from the Home, Hugh and Lindberg, labored like field hands all through the hot morning. Lucius and Sid helped a little, as did Chris and I, but it took the two younger men to do most of the pulling and jerking and cutting of the vines. Tenacious? I've never seen anything like it. It was caught in every window blind, between every two porch floorboards, even in and around the bricks of the foundation.

I went up the back steps cautiously. They call FairAcres "The House of Fallen Women," and with good reason. Somebody—usually a woman—falls nearly every day, and too often breaks a bone. I've learned to walk as though I'm stepping between eggs. I could pull some of the kudzu loose from the banisters, but the vine criss-crossed the steps in a way that defied me. I jerked and pulled, but didn't make much progress.

"Better let me get that, ma'am. That's a stubborn sucker," said Lindberg.

"Shucks!" said Hugh. "If these ladies weren't here I'd tell you what kinda sucker that thing is." He wiped his face on his sleeve and gave a jerk at a hefty tendril that had wound itself around the slats of a window blind. He jerked again, and the shutter came loose from the window.

"Oh, my gosh!" he said. "Look at that! You knew I wuz talkin' about you, didn't you? The way this stuff takes over and holds on, I think it's alive!"

"Sure it's alive," laughed Lindberg. "It grew, didn't it?"

"I don't mean that kind of alive," said Hugh. He looked at me, and I knew what he meant—that there seemed to be a malevolent consciousness in this creeper, this overly persistent, seizing member of the vegetable kingdom. I looked at the leaves in my hand and threw them down. Hateful vine!

"Let's take a break," I shouted to the others.

I had talked Mrs. Preston, in FairAcres' kitchen, into fixing a Thermos of iced tea and ten sandwiches for me. She was nice enough not to ask any questions. I had brought paper cups and plates, and we sat on the cleared steps and ate. Chris, Sidney, and Lucius looked as tired as I felt, and we weren't really doing much of the work.

"Don't you think we should call it a day?" I asked everyone in general.

"Oh, come on, Hattie. We can get the house clear in another hour. Don't you all think so?" Lucius looked at our two young companions.

"Maybe so," said Lindberg. "Thank God it's got a tin roof, and not shingles. "C'mon, Hugh. Grab that ladder."

What took most of their time on the roof were the dormer windows—three of them. We stood and watched the windows emerge from their burial in the greenery.

"You know," I said to Sidney, "I have a silly notion that those little windows are smiling!"

He smiled and agreed. "I would say it's a happier house than it was this morning."

"It's bound to be," I said, looking at the gingerbread trim and the fancy spindles of the banisters, the wide front door, and the windows with twelve panes, some of the glass so old it was wavy. "Now the house is alive again...Sidney, do you think we're trespassing?"

"Technically, maybe. Legally, maybe. Morally, no. As Lucius said, it's better than letting the house get 'et up.' We're not going inside or removing anything. Nothing but hurtful vines."

"I intend to find the owner as soon as I can," I assured them.

We talked of burning the mountains of green stuff that we had piled in several parts of the yard, but decided against it. Lucius paid off the young men, exacting a promise of secrecy from them, and we walked home wearily.

"I'll pay you my part of their wages, Lucius, as soon as I can get up the strength to find my pocketbook and open it," I said. "Whew! I'm dragging. I'm too old for this kind of good-deed stuff."

"Aren't we all!" Chris agreed heartily.

There's a new supermarket on the edge of Drayton, not too far from The Home, where we go sometimes to stock up on soft drinks and snacks. We go on days when we feel full of vim and vigor—able to push a cart up and down the aisles of the enormous place.

I'm told that one of our residents, Austin Craver, got fed up after a vain search for what he wanted at the supermarket. A big, nice man, a baritone who sings with gusto in our chapel choir, Austin finally stopped his cart in the middle of the Piggly Wiggly and shouted in his loudest voice:

"WHERE ARE THE POTATO CHIPS?"

He succeeded in getting help. In fact, help came running from all parts of the store.

Oh, dear, how we miss the retailing of old, where you went into a medium-sized store—sometimes called a "Mercantile Establishment, Groceries and Sundries" and probably the same store your parents frequented—told a clerk what you wanted, and he brought it to you pleasantly and promptly.

Or better still was when you could phone your order in, and perhaps say, "Tell Jason I won't be here, so ask him to please put the perishables in the refrigerator." You'd get a bill at the end of the month, and you mailed a check. No standing in line at the checkout counter with six people in front of you trying to pay with credit cards, food stamps, checks that need approving, or not-enough cash. Ah, me. Those *were* the good old days.

5

Arthur's News

June 28th

Thank God we can laugh. Existence at a retirement home—any kind of old folks' home—would be pretty miserable without that life-saving thing that a benevolent providence built into most people: a sense of humor.

Without it we would live in dread or fright or sorrow a good part of the time. We know there is an end to our short road—and that's a mystery—but it's the perils on the road that frighten us most: whether we will have a stroke like Mrs. So-and-So, whose mouth will droop hideously for the rest of her life, and who is pitifully frustrated by not being able to get out the right words; or whether osteoporosis or a fall will render us cripples, members of the large wheelchair brigade we have here.

We have the sadness of seeing deterioration in each other. "Have you noticed how he (or she) is failing?" That's a remark that is heard almost daily. I've begun to hate the word "failing." We witness decline—slow or fast, mental or physical—in people we have come to know and like, and that's vexing to the spirit. We want to cry out against it. We want to do something about it, and can't.

So, it's no wonder that we grab at every slightest chance to giggle or laugh out loud—even, alas, at someone else's expense sometimes.

For instance, Jerry Mosimann—a nice man, a quiet, gentle widower—never bothered anybody. His doctor decided he needed an operation. It was done in the hospital, but they brought him to our infirmary after two days for recuperation. The young, rather inexperienced doctor decided that, because of the nature of the operation, Jerry needed hormones, and he prescribed them.

Well sir (as my grandmother used to say, no matter who she was talking to), in a few days a metamorphosis took place in Jerry Mosimann's frail body. The hormones started raging.

He wore nothing but old-fashioned night shirts. They stopped half-way down his legs and had slits in the sides. His wife had made them for him. They were beautifully sewn, and very full so as not to bind him.

Well sir, they billowed out as the little man raced up and down the halls chasing the nurses! Sometimes he'd catch one in the treatment room or somewhere and start pawing her. She'd have to run for help, yelling for somebody to get him back to bed and tie him down!

Poor Mr. Mosimann. We shouldn't have laughed at him, but we couldn't help it. The doctor quickly decided to discontinue the hormones.

I hope the patient never found out why, or remembered the details. But oh, what a good laugh he gave us. Praise the Lord!

July 3rd

I was walking through the lobby, admiring the flower arrangement on the table under the mirror. Our house-keeper is a wizard with a few kumquat leaves and a handful of mums. I was feeling good in my new, two-piece fuchsia knit until, all of a sudden, a rasping voice called out: "For Lord's sake, Hattie, pull your skirt down in front!"

It was Geneva Tinken, sitting in one of the lounge chairs.

I glanced in the mirror. Sure enough, "pot-itis" had taken over again, and my knitted skirt was hiked in front and drooped behind. Nothing looks tackier.

A clothing company could make a mint if they came out with skirts two inches longer in front, for "potted ladies." Also, I think all clothes for old ladies should have long sleeves. With most of us, the skin on our arms hangs down in scallops.

I gave the front of my skirt a jerk and went on my way, not bothering to thank Geneva. I chuckled to myself, recalling Paul's priceless description, "...stinkin' old coot!"

July 5th

Well, aren't I the cat's meow! I have joined the technological revolution and gotten a word processor! Today I inaugurated it with a letter to Henrietta. Here's a copy:

Dear Retta—

Guess what? I have bought myself a word processor! And my first project is this letter to you. There are many puzzling things. For instance, they have dared to put the apostrophe in a different place! (I thought the typing keyboard was sacrosanct, but no.) I live with the fear that what I write will vanish from the screen before I can get it on a printed page, if I press the wrong key. Whew!

My daughter Nancy and her daughter Tricia got me into this. They were visiting last week and asked to read some of the notes I've made about retirement home living. They laughed and were complimentary, and said I MUST (I can do capitals, but I don't know how to do italics yet) put the "jottings" together in better form. Nancy took me processor shopping the next day. (Thank goodness they have come way down in price.)

The best thing about this contraption: you can back up and correct mistakes without the mess of eraser or white-out. With the number of errors I make, that's a considerable blessing. I only wish the machine could really live up to its name and process the words at their source—in my head—arranging them neatly and cogently before they hit the screen-nnnnnnnnnn...There it goes! I'll leave all those n's to show you that if you breathe too hard on a key, it takes off. You have to have the touch of a butterfly.

I have had quite an adventure lately—"the mystery of the abandoned cottage." You will have to read about it when you come down, which I hope will be QUITE SOON.

Much love,
Hattie

July 7th

I have called Amelia Easley's number several times, and finally today she answered. Said Hilton Head had been great.

"When are you coming to see me?" she asked. "It's your turn. You owe me."

"I know, but my car is being worked on. As soon as I get it back, I'll come over. But meantime, I want to ask you something."

I told her about Kudzu Kottage and about our interest in trying to save the appealing little place. When I asked if she knew who owned it, she said she had an idea but wasn't sure. She said that she would find out and get back to me. I think I got her interested too.

Something else has come up that has me worried. It

involves that nice Arthur Priest. After Angela Pryor left, he went right back to being his old polite, happy, helpful self; but today, when he came to see what was making my garbage disposal act up, he was quiet, almost morose. He found the trouble with the appliance, fixed it, and then let the disposal grind up a few ice cubes to clean out the works. (I never would have thought of that. He knows *more* good tricks.)

Finally, after not being able to get much conversation out of him, I said, "Is anything the matter, Arthur?"

He nodded, but said, "It's nothing about anyone here. I'd better not talk about it, ma'am. Is there anything else you have that needs workin' on?"

When I said no, he started packing up his tools. His young face looked so clouded and miserable, I couldn't stand it.

"Now, Arthur, sit down. You always seem to be enjoying life, but not today. I know something must be wrong. Maybe I can help."

"No ma'am, I don't think you can this time. I know you would if you could." He waited a minute and then said, "You see, Dollie has just found out that she's gonna have another baby."

"Why, that's wonderful! Maybe you'll get a girl this time."

He shrugged and looked wretched. I tried again. "Your two fine and handsome boys would probably love a beautiful little sister."

He gave a weak smile. "When we first got married we talked about havin' three kids... It would be nice to have a girl, if we had anywhere to put her. You see, Miz McNair, there're three of us in the bedroom now, and Artie sleeps on the sofa-bed in the livin' room. There's not an inch of room for a crib."

I remembered that tiny house, the cramped room where we had sat. "Well, I suppose you'll just have to find another place, Arthur. That's all you can do."

"That's easy to say, ma'am, if you'll excuse me. But on what I make here, I'm lucky to be able to rent that little ol' trailer. And there'll be another mouth to feed."

I don't know what he makes. It must be a pittance... There was a bit of an awkward silence, and Arthur got up to leave.

"How are your lessons coming with Miss Canfield?" I asked.

"Real good." He brightened up. "My readin' is up to fifth-grade level now."

That didn't sound so wonderful to me. "What grade will it have to reach for you to take the driver's test?"

"The eighth, I think."

So it will be a while longer before he can even try for a better job. Poor Arthur. I gave him some candy to take to his boys and told him I'd give his plight some thought.

6

Mr. Andrew Hoskins

July 20th

When I first came here, Helen and Henry Durant were a sweet couple, utterly devoted. She is slightly crippled, so he kept his arm under hers, guiding her everywhere. Alas, that old devil Alzheimer's attacked him and worked its miserable change. Very soon he had to be moved to a room in the infirmary. Now their roles are reversed. I see her twice a day limping over there, tiredly, to do what she can for him.

At first Henry was wretched. He told Helen that nobody would talk to him; but one day she found him smiling, elated. "I've found a friend," he said. "Nicest fellow. He agrees with everything I say!"

The nurse called Helen out in the hall and showed her a

long mirror on the wall. "He sat in his wheelchair in front of that mirror for an hour this morning, talking and nodding. He seemed so happy!"

Felix, another Alzheimer's patient in the infirmary, was bored and unhappy until he found that he could keep busy pushing wheelchair-bound patients around. The only thing is, most of them don't want to be pushed at all, especially by a fellow who charges around wildly and bumps into everything.

One day when Felix's wife came to see him, he wasn't in his room, nor was he careening around the halls pushing unwilling patients. She couldn't find him anywhere. Two nurses joined the search, and they finally located him in a room that was far from his room.

That wasn't all. It was a double room, and there was a woman in the other bed who also didn't belong there. Both of them were peacefully sleeping under the sheets, but fully clothed, even to their shoes!

One of the reasons most of us have chosen this place is that FairAcres has an infirmary, and yet we dread the thought that we will probably end our days in that part of the "institution." We don't like to think of the infirmary. We hate the name of it, and we avoid looking at that brick extension when we walk around the campus.

My conscience bothers me for not spending more time visiting people in the infirmary. I know there are many of them who need cheering up, but by the time I get to their rooms I need cheering up. Was there ever a more depressing place? I think not. Many of the poor patients are sitting in wheelchairs in the halls, most with heads hanging down and mouths hanging open.

There is one woman who reaches out and grabs my skirt as I walk by and begs, "Please get me out of here! Please take me home!" The nurses say she doesn't know who she is or where home is. Nevertheless, the tone of her plea kills me.

I'm sure the patients are well taken care of. In fact, in one respect, in my opinion, their care is too good. I mean those times when the ones in their nineties, completely *non compos mentis,* are given antibiotics. When I was growing up, pneumonia was called "the old folks' friend."

I talked to my doctor about it recently. He admitted that pneumonia causes a fairly painless death. "But we are trained, in medicine," he said, "to fight death with every possible weapon." Ah, there's the rub. More attention is paid to the length of life than to the quality of it.

As I read somewhere: "Modern medicine has not really prolonged life—not *real* life; it has just lengthened the process of dying."

August 5th

Rose Hibben has bad hay fever. Poor thing. In late summer and early fall her nose and eyes are usually streaming from ragweed and other grasses. It has gotten her nose in such a fix that almost anything can make it run, even when ragweed season is over. A two-degree drop in temperature can start the dripping.

As if that weren't enough, Rose also suffers from a weak bladder. I heard her say one day, "In the next life, if I can just have a dry nose and a strong bladder, I will be satisfied."

Yesterday I asked Rose if she were going to her cousin's daughter's wedding in Charleston. "No, I can't," she said, shaking her head sadly. "I want to go, but I don't dare. By the time I drive down there and sit through the wedding it will be two hours, and I can't *go* two hours."

"Oh, Rose, " I said, "you *know* that big Episcopal church has rest rooms."

"Yes," she said, "but I don't know where they are, and I don't want to go scrambling in front of people in the pew, stepping on their toes, trying to get out...I love Dorothy's daughter, and I don't want to rain on her parade—" She put her hand to her mouth and whispered, "or pee on it!"

This weak bladder business is one of the most persistent and embarrassing ailments here. I well know. It governs nearly everything I do. I get *so* aggravated. The only thing that slows down my wrath is thinking about the people who can't "go" at all—the ones who have to be hooked up to those dialysis machines two or three times a week.

There's a pretty actress on TV who advertises pads that are cleverly named. I may have to break down and "depend" on them, but I hate the thought. I wonder if that actress uses them. She seems so young.

Speaking of rest rooms, I'm an authority. The public ones on the interstate highways are a blessing. Before they came along I sometimes had to suffer, because Sam wouldn't stop at a filling station unless he needed gas. "I'm not going to use someone's facilities for nothing," he'd say, virtuously. If I was absolutely desperate he'd stop, but he'd buy Cokes and potato chips or candy, whether we wanted them or not.

Last spring my youngest son, Ray, and his wife were driving me to a grandson's wedding in Atlanta. At my request we were taking secondary roads so that I could go through Madison and Washington, Georgia—my very favorite towns in all the world—and as usual, my plight came upon me suddenly. Ray stopped at the very next filling station. (He didn't inherit his father's strange reticences.) I ran inside the station, only to find an "Out of Order" sign on the LADIES' door. The clerk saw my distress and called me over to the counter. "We put up two Port-o-Lets today, outside and to the left. You can use one of those if you want to."

I thanked the dear girl and dashed outside, saying, "Any Port-o-Let in a storm!"

My mother would be shocked that I would dare to write about such things. She was painfully old-fashioned. She did her dressing and undressing in her clothes closet. I doubt if my father ever saw her *en déshabillé,* or even half-way disrobed. Anything that happened to produce four children must have taken place in the black dark!

According to Mama, her mother was even more modest. When a group of ladies in that Victorian era were having tea, and one of them had to "go," she wouldn't dream of saying so. She would say, "Excuse me, please. I have to step aside."

The false modesty of those times reached laughable extremes, but to me they were nicer extremes than the ones being reached today, when anything goes—when the shock level has plunged to an all-time low. I'd rather have people saying they have to "step aside" than to see on television what they're stepping aside for.

L.A. Law was an interesting show at times, but we followed the lawyers to the rest room and heard (almost saw) the unzipping. I often wonder what my mother would think of the slobbering kisses and the sex scenes that usually followed.

Once, when Mama was visiting us, a forester friend of Sam's dropped in. We began to talk about our local trees, and I complained because Christmas was coming and my large holly tree in the front yard showed no signs of producing a single berry.

"Maybe it's a female tree," said the forester, "and is in need of a male tree nearby."

Mama turned to me and whispered behind her hand, "Even *trees?* I think that's disgusting!"

Some of us were talking one day about our mothers, and Rose said that her mother's naiveté was a constant source of merriment in her family. Once her brother brought a fraternity brother home to spend the night. They came in from a party showing signs of having bent their elbows too freely. When they'd gone to bed the mother shook her head and said, "Those boys have had entirely too much to drink. I'm sure they'll have lay-overs in the morning!"

August 9th

Amelia Easley came to see me yesterday and told me that she has tracked down the owner of Kudzu Kottage.

"I was pretty sure, from your description, that it belongs to Mr. Andrew Hoskins, and it does. Apparently he pays the taxes on it and then forgets it."

"But that's so stupid! He could sell it or rent it to someone who would take care of it—"

"Sure. It makes no sense. Nothing that Mr. Hoskins does these days makes sense. His wife died a few years ago, and since then he doesn't seem to care about anything on God's earth. He owns some really good pieces of property in Drayton, but he's letting them go to wrack and ruin. Just doesn't care. He won't even keep himself looking decent. He's becoming a hermit."

"Oh, dear! The four of us were so hoping that the house was owned by somebody from out of town, who had maybe forgotten about it. Somebody we could appeal to, to rescue it."

I told her briefly about Arthur and his family and their predicament. "There's that house just sitting there, looking forlorn—and when I think of what Arthur and Dollie could make of it—and how they'd love it!"

"Well, you can appeal to Mr. Hoskins if you want to, but I don't hold out much hope. Richard calls him 'the old goat.' And I'll tell you something else, Hattie, these days he looks like he might smell like a goat. When I think of how he looked when Miss Annie was alive…She always kept him 'spiffed out,' spic and span."

"Are there any children?"

"No. The two of them were just wrapped up in each other—and now I guess he feels lost. In a way I'm sorry for him, but Richard says he needs a swift kick. Says he's letting the town down, the way all his properties are deteriorating. Some of them are eyesores and fire hazards."

"Does he have an office?" I asked.

"Yes. It's upstairs over Spear's Store on Town Square. I think he's there sometimes, but I understand he's holed up in his house a good part of the time."

"If we were to decide to try to see him, which place do you think we should go to?"

Amelia shrugged. "Honestly, Hattie, I don't know. Either way, I'm afraid you're wasting your efforts. But I admire you for trying."

I persisted and got from her directions for locating his house. It's a good thing I did, because most of Drayton's streets are winding and pointless, leading nowhere— somebody called them paved-over cow paths—and Christine and I would have wandered around for an hour today. As it was, we almost ended up in the lumber yard.

I had talked to my other three conspirators about approaching Mr. Hoskins and trying to get him to rent his cottage to the Priest family for a nominal fee (the same that they were paying for the trailer I hoped), with the understanding that they would improve the house and grounds in every possible way.

"It sounds great to me," Lucius had said, and Sidney agreed.

"And to me," said Chris. "But, Hattie, I think a delegation of four is too large."

"She's right," said Sidney. "Hattie, why don't you and Chris take on the job—" he smiled and added, "with the advice and consent of the menfolks, of course. I believe you two ladies could do a better job of persuading…and appealing…"

So it was that Chris and I set out with great trepidation, in my old Buick. We had tried to phone Mr. Hoskins but had learned that his phones, at both the house and office, had been disconnected.

We decided to try to beard the lion in his home den. After two or three wrong turns, we finally located 318 Oleander Street and swung into the driveway of a large Victorian house with porches around three sides, rounded at the corners. I imagine it was impressive and inviting at one time; but now the white paint was peeling, and the house looked desolate.

We waded through last year's leaves and fallen limbs in the unkempt yard and went up the steps to a porch that apparently had not felt the stroke of a broom "in a coon's age." We rang the bell three times and could hear it pealing inside, but no one came.

Undaunted, we wound our way back to the town's square
and found a parking place. (They are easy to find on the
square these days, with most shopping being done at the
mall on the edge of town.) We located the steep stairway on
the left of Spear's Store and trudged up.

Whew! What a climb! Those old stores had high ceilings.
Chris is about two years my junior, but she got winded too.
We panted a little, and stopped twice, but made it to the
top. There, we found ourselves in front of a door that said,

ANDREW P. HOSKINS
Real Estate & Insurance

Suddenly we were daunted. Maybe it was being winded
that did it, but all at once I had cold feet, and I could tell
Christine felt the same way. This old man didn't know us.
He owed us nothing. Were we being nervy as all get-out, to
try to tell him what to do with his property?

But we had come this far. We had to try. I gave a very
tentative knock on the door. Nothing happened. I knocked
again, a little harder. We heard something that sounded like
a halfhearted, "Come in," and in we went.

I won't try to describe the messy office or the messy old
man in detail. Suffice it to say that both could have done
with some cleaning, and both looked forlorn.

Mr. Hoskins had retained enough of his good raising to
rise from his desk when he saw we were two females, and to
offer us chairs, but he gave no hint of welcome. His
expression seemed to say, "What in God's name have I done
to deserve this?"

We introduced ourselves, and with Chris's nod of encouragement I launched into the reason for our visit, with no preliminaries.

"Mr. Hoskins, I believe you own a house on Boundary Lane, not far from FairAcres Home, where we live."

He thought for a minute, turned away from his cluttered desk, and swiveled in his chair to a nearby cabinet. From it he pulled a large ledger, opened it, and turned some pages.

"Six-room bungalow. 402 Boundary Lane. That it?"

We nodded.

"What about it?" he said, turning back to the open ledger. "I bought that place at a sheriff's sale in 1978. I've paid the taxes every year on the due date. What's the matter?"

"Nothing's the matter, really..." said Chris. "I mean—"

"Yes, something *is* the matter, Mr. Hoskins," I burst in. I proceeded to tell him that he was letting a perfectly nice little house go back to the jungle. I tried to paint a vivid picture of what was happening to it; and suddenly I realized that the more I talked, the redder his face was getting. He took off his glasses and squinted at me. This made his wrinkled face look almost sinister.

Finally, he held up his hand. "Hold on there, madam. Just what is your interest in *my* property?"

There was so much scorn and hostility in the question that I was taken aback. I stuttered an attempted reply.

"Well...y-you s-s-see—" Oh, dear, I thought. We're dead before we even get to our good reason.

Chris tried to step into the breach. "We're not interested for ourselves, Mr. Hoskins. You see, there's a deserving young couple...." She went on to tell him about Arthur and Dollie and their children, about how desperately they needed a bigger place to live. The more she talked, the more he scowled. He rose up and glared.

"I will thank you ladies to stay out of my business," he said, his voice shaking a little. "I bid you good day."

We got out of there without another word. We went down the steps four times faster than we had come up them. We held on to each other all the way to the car, not speaking. My heart was pounding and my face burning as I sat gripping the steering wheel trying to calm down before turning the ignition.

"If I were a drinking woman," said Chris, "I'd go to a bar and have a double Scotch right now."

"The *old goat!*" was all I could think of to say.

Later

I went to walk on our campus late this afternoon. The colors of the sunset were so outrageously brilliant that when they finally faded I had a feeling—probably a silly feeling—that they left the sky blushing in the remaining dusk.

I felt better after the privilege of that gorgeous sight. Chris and I had done what we could. Maybe something can still be worked out for Arthur and his little family. *Dum spiro spero.*

"I will thank you ladies to stay out of my business…"

Also, I couldn't stay too glum after some of the things I heard at the supper table. As usual, laughter had a very healing effect. A sample:

There are six women and two men at the table, this go-round. The men try to sit side by side. Edwin says that's for protection against too much "she-she" talk.

And later on one of the women said, "I asked my cousin Ellen, who's eighty-one, if she was making any arrangements about going to a retirement home, and she said, 'No. I've told my girls just to put me in a corner and let me drool.'" We all laughed at the image. I'm glad we can laugh instead of cry!

August 24th

We have a "Country Store" here at The Home, a small room off the lobby where we can buy candy, ice cream, stamps, toothpaste, and the like. Whenever I need something, the store seems to be closed. I haven't learned the odd hours set by the attendants, all volunteer residents.

Today, however, I caught it open.

I was sitting at one of the tiny tables, happily licking away at a cone of Chocolate Swirl, when Angus McLeod came in. He took a look at my ice cream and said, "I'll have one of those." Then he sat down at my table, which surprised me.

A widower, he is a quiet and reticent man. A good part of his reticence is due, I think, to a difficulty he has in speaking. He has had serious throat trouble, and it affected his larynx. His voice sounds hoarse, but at close range, when he doesn't have to strain so, he is completely understandable.

"I'm intrigued by your very Scottish name, Mr. McLeod," I said.

"Are you? That's nice." He smiled and added shyly, "My middle name is Dougald."

"Angus Dougald McLeod! Why, I can almost hear the bagpipes! 'Scots wha hae wi' Wallace bled,' and 'aw that.' Were your people from the Highlands?"

"Indeed they were. They came over in 1774 with Flora Macdonald."

"*Really?* It has always stirred my imagination—the story of a sizable group of people leaving their homes and striking out for an unknown land, all out of loyalty to a woman!"

"Not just an ordinary woman," he said. "Flora must have been a dilly!"

"So she must," I agreed. "However, I believe I read that she went back to Scotland after a few years, but most of her followers stayed in North Carolina."

"That's right," Angus said, stopping to catch a drip from his cone. " 'Twas warmer than 'the Heelands,' and offered more opportunities."

"I'm interested because I have Scottish ancestors, too," I told him. "My great-grandmother was Euphemia McNeill, of Ellerbe Springs, North Carolina."

"Oh, yes. In Richmond County."

"That's right. Anyway, I've been told that those particular McNeills came to America from the Kintyre peninsula. I don't know much about them, except that my ancestress Euphemia was called Effie."

"Better than Euphie!" said Mr. McLeod, with a twinkle, and I readily agreed.

"Speaking of Flora's brood," he said, "have you ever seen their church, Old Bethesda, outside of Aberdeen, North Carolina?"

"No, but I've heard about it. It's around two hundred years old, isn't it?"

"More than that. The names on the tombstones will make you think you're in an Edinburgh cemetery: MacThis and MacThat, all over the place."

"Is the church used now?"

"Oh, no. We moderns can't put up with drafts and no heat and no electricity. We built a warm, tight, air-conditioned structure about a mile away, years ago. But my grandfather attended Old Bethesda—under duress. He used to tell me about those two-hour services in winter, with no heat of any kind in the church. Said it made him shiver just to think about them. If you were about eighty years old, and sickly, you could bring a hot brick wrapped in a cloth, for your feet, in very cold weather."

Angus continued his reminiscence. "Grandpa said musical instruments were frowned upon. Brother Somebody—probably Brother *Mac*Somebody—had a tuning fork. He would 'heist' the tune, and you sang seven or eight verses, mostly doleful. There was a line in one of the hymns that particularly scared Grandpa as a boy. The hymn was describing Heaven: 'Where congregations ne'er break up, and sabbaths last for aye.' He said that sounded more like The Bad Place to him!"

We had a good laugh over that. Poor little boy!

"I'd like to have known your grandfather," I said.

"I wish you could have. Salt of the earth. Strong, steady, a little stern—but with a twinkle in his eye…He told me about his mother, my great-grandmother, who was such a bluestocking Presbyterian that she wouldn't let her children go for a walk on Sunday—except in the cemetery! And tight about money! When she cleaned out her medicine chest every spring, she would shake her head at any leftover medicine. And sometimes she would drink some of it, rather than throw it out. 'Well, it might do me some good,' she'd say. 'It cost a great deal of money.'"

I enjoyed my session with Angus Dougald McLeod. I'm sure there are other quiet, retiring souls here who have good stories in their backgrounds. Maybe I will visit the Country Store more often, and encourage some confidences over cones of Chocolate Swirl.

7

Miss Minna

August 28th

Only three more days of August left, thank goodness. I can hardly wait for October...And there I go again, wishing my days away. I haven't got that many days left. I should hoard each one, boiling hot or not.

But August really outdoes itself in uncomfortable-ness, it seems to me. In fact, last night I scribbled this rhyme on a scrap of paper:

AUGUST—SCHMAUGUST
August is a messy month
With skeeters, flies, and fleas,
With thunderstorms and gale alarms
And weeds up to your knees.

The mercury climbs up the tube
>   And tempers start to snap.
Spirits wilt like lettuce leaves
>   And even lovers scrap.

If I were Augustus Caesar
>   Resting in my shroud
And knew this month was named for me
>   I wouldn't feel too proud.

September 5th

Soon after I came to this place I discovered that we have a resident genius, aged eighty-two—a woman who can make a piano sing and cry and give forth melodies that seem to come from a better world! The same melodies played by anyone else do not seem to have the feeling and sweetness she evokes. Truly, they do not. (And I am somewhat of an authority, having taken piano lessons for twelve years and having been encouraged to consider making a career of it. But I'm glad I didn't. I wasn't that good, and I was better as wife and mother.)

I was passing through our lobby when I heard a marvelous sound coming from the large parlor, the one with the baby grand Steinway that someone bequeathed to FairAcres. It was Chopin's "Raindrop Prelude," and it was getting a masterful rendition. I slipped quietly into a chair and drank in the lilting beauty of the notes, so perfectly played. Who in the world? It must be a visitor.

But no—as it turned out, it was a resident, Miss Minna McKenzie, who had spent her life in Drayton as a music teacher. When she finished the prelude I introduced myself to her, and we talked for a while about Chopin—about the particularly beautiful numbers he wrote while spending a winter on an island (was it Majorca?) with George Sand.

"I understand," said Miss Minna, "that he nearly froze to death that winter in the old, old house they rented." With a little quirk to her mouth, she added softly, "Served him right!"

Miss Minna is tiny, and her hands are so small it is hard to believe what they can accomplish on a keyboard. She's lovely to look at: soft white hair kept long and twisted into a French knot in the back. Two little ivory combs try to capture all the strands, but two or three tendrils always manage to curl down the back of her neck.

The kind of pink-cheeked prettiness that some old ladies are lucky enough to have, she has in abundance. With violet eyes and a gentle expression, Miss Minna is something! My first thought after I learned that she was "Miss" McKenzie, was: Why in the world didn't some man grab her?

We hit it off right away and decided to try to play duets as soon as we could locate some interesting ones in our music stacks. This we have been doing from time to time, to my great joy.

Playing with that sweet and gifted lady has been the very brightest spot of my sojourn here at The Home. We are even considering giving a concert some night after supper.

A number of residents have asked us to. We could have folding chairs put up in the lobby, near the large parlor.

I hope we can persuade Mr. Detwiler to have somebody work on the Steinway. The old instrument is great (so much better than the ones put out by the company today), but it is in need of a tuning job and pedal work.

Gusta Barton seems obsessed with thoughts of her demise and her burial service. Today she said, "It'll be in my home church, but there'll be just a pitiful handful of mourners. Nearly everybody I ever knew is dead."

Rose Hibben came up with a suggestion. "Gusta, you could tell your son that when you die, you want him to put out the word that there will be door prizes at the funeral."

Gusta's face lit up. "That's an idea!" she said.

Oh, my!!!

September 11th

Miss Minna and I played our duets after supper last night. To my surprise, all the folding chairs were occupied, as well as the upholstered chairs and sofas in the lobby.

The piano had been tuned nicely. We (especially I) had practiced a lot, and we really sounded pretty good. She was "primo" to my "secundo," which was a help to me. We played two numbers, a Mendelssohn and then a Schubert, and both went quite well, I thought. We had found an arrangement of Scott Joplin's "Maple Leaf Rag" for four hands and used it as an encore. That made a hit. I could see people swaying and tapping their toes. All of them asked us to play again soon. Maybe we will.

We call each other by our first names here—except for Dr. Browning and Minna McKenzie. Everybody calls her "Miss Minna." Maybe it's because, as the music teacher, that's what she was called in Drayton for most of her life. Southern towns tend to retain some of their old-fashioned ways; also, the name seems to fit her. Utterly gentle and kind, there is yet an air of—not haughtiness; maybe dignity is the word. She holds her head up, and you don't slap her on the back or get too familiar.

But, oh, how dear she can be when she likes you! Mixed with her good taste and gentility is a delicious sense of humor. I was completely captivated by her from our first meeting, and I said so to Amelia Easley who had actually taken piano lessons from her.

Amelia is a darling—much like her mother, Lucy, who was my best friend in college. As soon as Lucy, who lives in Asheville, wrote her daughter, who lives in Drayton, that I had moved into FairAcres, Amelia came right over, bringing a bottle of Harvey's Bristol Cream and a batch of homemade cheese biscuits, enough for me to invite the whole hall in for a "githerin'" the next day. It's lovely when you're seventy-nine and find, to your surprise, that you have started a productive and fast friendship with someone decades younger.

"I thought you and Miss Minna would hit it off," Amelia said. "I remember sitting by her on the piano bench during my lessons and enjoying the faint scent of her toilet water and the grace of her hands. And when she praised my playing, which wasn't often," Amelia laughed, "I loved her voice."

"Ah, her voice," I agreed, "and her smile! Anyone that pretty must have had beau, Amelia. Why didn't she marry?"

"I asked Mama that once. She told me the story of Miss Minna's romance. It's sad. Are you sure you want to hear it?"

"Oh, yes. But first, look." I pointed to the sun shining on the tall pines that reached to my second-floor windows. "The sun has come out at last. Let's walk to the pond. There's a good place to sit, and we can feed the ducks."

I'm grateful to whoever landscaped the grounds at FairAcres. There are peaceful paths for walking and several swings and gazebos on the banks of a small lake where we can sit and watch the ducklings swim in seeming formation behind their proud mamas. Because there are so many of us who bring them bread crumbs and scraps from the dining room, these ducks are probably the most overfed creatures in South Carolina.

Amelia and I settled into chairs in a gazebo. "Now tell me," I said, "about Miss Minna."

"Well, Mama said Miss Minna had a string of beaus. Said they hung around 'like Grant hung around Richmond!' And then it narrowed down to one serious swain, Grainger Pendarvis."

"Why didn't she marry him?"

"It really looked as if she was going to. They were seen everywhere together—church, the library, picnics, the drugstore—"

"Was he good-looking?"

"Very. Tall and well-built. Mama said he had been an All-Southern football player in college. He got a good job at the bank, and Miss Minna grew more radiant by the day."

"What happened?"

"Miss Minna got sick. Let's see, what did she have? Oh, I remember. It was glandular fever. I think they call it mononucleosis now. She had a bad case...had to be put to bed for about three months. Just at that time a new family moved to town—the Harrises—with a daughter named Marguerite. She got a job at the bank and soon set her cap for Grainger."

"Oh, dear! She *got* him?"

"Yes, she got him. She wasn't nearly as pretty as Miss Minna, but had ten times as much shrewdness and determination. It was just poor Miss Minna's bad luck to be bedridden right at that time—although I don't know whether or not she would have fought hard for him if she'd been well. She's so gentle.

"Apparently she had gobs of chances to get married later, but I guess she was a one-man woman. Mama said Grainger *was* a knockout as a young man. Anybody else would have been a comedown for her, I suppose. Poor thing. She didn't have the money to go away, and just had to tough it out."

"I wonder if Grainger regretted his marriage?"

"Oh, yes. Even I could tell that. I'd see him downtown sometimes, in the bank or the post office or the drugstore. Saddest-looking man I ever saw."

We were quiet for a while, throwing crumbs to the ducks and ruminating on the exigencies of fate.

September 16th

Talked with Henrietta last night—her name is moving up the list—so I wrote her today. Here's a copy.

> Dear Retta,
>
> I've had you on my mind this morning, after our good talk last night, knowing that you have to decide soon whether or not to hibernate in a home. You know I'd love to have you here, but am afraid to encourage you, in case you should find—too late— that you're not happy with the choice.
>
> Sometimes I'm reminded of you when I'm working a crossword puzzle, which I do daily. I think the mental exercise gets a little rust off the wheels, even when I cheat a bit. (Who in the world could be expected to know another word for "mussitates" or "lachesis"?) Anyway, when I get stuck, I'd like to be able to pick your brain, and take advantage of your word-love and word-knowledge.
>
> I thought of you recently when I came upon a Greek word: *entheos,* which was translated as "God in us." I'm not sure, but I think our word

"enthusiasm" comes from *entheos,* from "God in us," and I find that intriguing. Do you?

These days I seem to be having a kind of love affair with words. I don't want to know all the words in the world and their definitions, just for knowing's sake. I want to know the beautiful words, the ones packed with interest and color and meaning.

If you were asked to name the three most beautiful words, what would you list? Probably the same three I would choose—the ones that name the virtues extolled in Corinthians: faith, hope, and love. "Charity," too, is pretty in sound and meaning. For just sound, I like "lilt," "intuitive," "amaryllis." I've read that the most euphonious words are the ones with the most "l's." "Amaryllis" to me sounds like water running out of a bottle!

At the other end of the scale are the ugly words, such as "belch," "pregnant," "nard," "gulch"...I don't like to spend time on them.

I will close with a "happening" from yesterday—true, I'll swear.

Mr. and Mrs. Culver have seen better days, mentally. I met them in the hall, right outside the dining room door. They looked slightly puzzled, and Mrs. Culver said to me, "Tell me, dear, is this lunch or early supper?"

"It's lunch," I replied.

"Then tell me, please," she said, lowering her voice and looking a bit distressed, "have we eaten it?"

Please write to me soon.

Love,
Hattie

September 19th

We were talking at lunch today about women's libbers, and Ethel McDill went into a diatribe. She said, "I don't want a lady dentist, a lady doctor, a lady accountant, or a lady preacher! And I don't want to be called Ms. or Chairperson. I want things like they *were,* when men were men and women were glad of it. We were glad to have doors opened for us, hats taken off in our presence, and seats given up for us. Poor women's libbers. Poor deprived creatures. I'm sorry for them. They don't know what they're missing!"

I said, "Amen, sister."

We went on to talk about The Old Days, about a sweeter time when there were hayrides and Christian Endeavor on Sunday nights and parlor games and singing around the piano. There was an innocence and a propriety that seem to be just about gone. Ah, me.

Again tonight I overheard Paul and Curtis talking on the terrace. (I'm going to have to stop sitting at that place in the library, I suppose. Doggone it!)

Curtis said, "Paul, you know that woman named Celia Thomas?"

"Yeah. Lives on D Hall. What about her?"

"I think she's got the hots for me."

"What? *Celia*? Oh come on, man."

"No, it's true. She's comin' on to me. I'm tellin' ya!"

After a minute Paul said, "Curtis, how old are you?"

"Eighty-five."

"Well, what I want to know is, why in God's name would she go out after an eighty-five-year-old when she could have someone who's only eighty-one? Like me?"

They chuckled over that for a while, and I returned to my room, thankful yet again for our long-lived sense of humor.

8

Indian Summer

Bad news from home. Another old friend has died—Lou Bettinger—a valued friend, loyal and fun. Sometimes I think all the best people are dead. Why am I not? Why do I continue to inhabit the planet? To use scarce oxygen, water, and food?

I can't do any more for my children. In fact, I could do much more for them dead. They will inherit enough money to bring a little joy into their work-a-day lives. Is there enough joy in mine to make my continuing to live any kind of a blessing? Enough of a blessing to postpone their inheritance?

Let's see...Joy. I enjoy eating food, which means that my tongue and palate get pleasure for a few seconds from one or two of the edibles that nourish me every day...I enjoy a good movie, and occasionally I come upon a good one among the miles of moving images that I watch too many of, on that box in a corner of my living room.

I enjoy good music, and am able, with today's electronics, to bask in an atmosphere of heavenly sounds whenever I'm in my home or car.

I enjoy good poetry, which is as close as my bookcase, and some of which I can actually call up from the depths of my memory, to break the monotony as I bathe or go to walk or drive along the highway.

There are people I enjoy being with—but not for too long at a time. I like to go home—or have them go home—so that I can think about what we said or did in peace and quiet.

So these are the joys. As I said above, are they enough of a reason for my long lingering among the upright? As the Preacher said in Ecclesiastes, "There is a time to be born and a time to die." I guess it's not my time yet. And I'd better not worry about it because, as the Psalmist said, "The judgments of the Lord are true and righteous altogether."

Perhaps it is this early fall, Indian Summer weather that has me in such a reflective mood. The trees portend autumn. There are still plenty of blooms around, however. The gardeners here (the resident gardeners, I mean, with their tiny plots—not the hired landscape people) go in for old-fashioned flowers: verbena, dusty miller, Sweet William...I wonder who Sweet William was. A lost love? A dear, gentle little son, immortalized by a doting green-thumbed mother?

Two people came in late to lunch yesterday. One of them asked one of the seated men, who had already started eating, to ask the blessing. He swallowed and, after a few seconds, said, "Bless the Lord, oh my soul, *and all that is within me,* bless His holy name. Amen."

September 26th

I like baseball. I like the sound of the ball hitting the bat—*thwack*—and seeing the batter sling his bat any old where and take off, to first or further. I slide the last three yards with him and am furious when sometimes the base umpire yells, "Out!"

When it comes time for a double play, I get close to the TV, but I can't make my head and eyes move fast enough to see everything that goes on. It is *so fast.* I will never understand how the players accomplish that feat, putting out two men faster than the speed of light.

When the season is winding down toward the World Series, I'm trapped. I sit up 'til nearly midnight sometimes, when the score is tied.

So...I like baseball; and I feel lucky that I can sit in my nice comfortable chair and watch those talented athletes on my good clear screen. But I'll tell you something, Dear Diary, I don't like to hear them talk. A few of them can speak decently, but I've heard some players being interviewed who sound as if they have a handful of wadding in their mouths. What a struggle it is to elicit from them even a fraction of an intelligible sentence.

"Yeah, we did awright, man! They had us down, y'know,
an' then we come back in th' eighth, y'know..."

"What do you think of your chances in the playoffs?"

"Well, y'know, we gonna try. We gonna give 'em hell,
y'know. Yeah, man. Hee-hee. We gonna give 'em hell, y'know."

I get so tired of "y'know," and not only from baseball
players. It's a plague! I decided today to try to write some
lines about it, and here's the result:

NEVERMO', Y'KNOW

No words were ever as overworked
    As these two words: "You know."
They punctuate each phrase that falls
    From the lips of Jane and Joe.

Kids from college, kids from slums,
    Kids both bright and slow,
They stick it in with every breath:
    "Y'know...y'know...y'know."

Oh, me, we've reached a pretty pass,
    Our culture's mighty low
When young folks can't communicate
    Without "y'know." Y'know?

If this had been the custom
    In the time of Edgar Poe,

D'you s'pose the raven would have quothed,
  "Nevermo', y'know"?

Or maybe Patrick Henry
    Would have muttered, very slow,
"You all give me liberty
    Or give me death, y'know."

I know one thing: it's tiresome.
    I may be square, but oh,
I'm weary of those wornout words.
    "Y'know" has GOT to go!

And speaking of baseball, another thing that bothers me
is the amount of spitting that goes on, and the way the men
spit—right straight out. So, being in a rhyming mood, I've
come up with some more doggerel:

P-TUI!
World Series games are lots of fun
    With noise and jubilation,
But I could wish there wouldn't be
    So much expectoration.

With bats in hand and wads in cheek,
    The men are mighty hitters,
But I wish they wouldn't try to prove
    They're also champion spitters!

September 28th

As I was walking down a hall in the infirmary I met a lady in a wheelchair. She put out her hand and stopped me.

"Honey," she said, "can you tell me how to get where I'm goin'?"

"Well, ma'am, where are you trying to go?"

"I don't know," she said cheerfully. "They haven't told me yet."

October 2nd

Late this afternoon on my after-supper stroll I saw at least six planes crisscrossing in the sky, leaving contrails that looked like a giant game of tic-tac-toe. The flyers were probably from the Charleston Air Force Base. What a way to end a glorious autumn day—for them, I mean, the pilots, playing around in a ceiling of October's bright blue weather! *And* for me, seeing such a sight!

As the sun set, over toward Orangeburg, it left a flaming palette of blending pinks and deep roses and fuchsias that was hard for my eyes to believe—one of those dazzling displays that almost scorch the eyeballs, and cannot be put down in mundane words.

To add to the display, all those crossing contrails turned bright pink, and the planes shone like polished sterling. I wondered if the pilots enjoyed it as much as I did. I wondered if one of them might be a budding poet and might try to draw the picture in words to warm a winter's night. I wondered what A. E. Housman would have done with it...and Whitman...and Wordsworth.

I don't believe the poets whose work I read, and groan over, in *The Atlantic* and *Harper's,* could make anything beautiful or touching out of that scene. They would have to find a way to "obscure it up." But I, "when on my couch I lie, in vacant or in pensive mood," like Wordsworth will treasure the memory of those pink contrails as they "flash upon the inward eye which is the bliss of solitude," as he treasured the flash of dancing daffodils.

My, I'm flowery tonight! Maybe I should bite on a pickle.

I'm reminded of my Aunt Nell, of that summer long ago when three of her sons—in their teens and early twenties—were in love at the same time. The air was full of sighs, of Wayne King's sugary music, of soft nothings being whispered over the telephone. Aunt Nell said the sweetness got so thick that she would have to go in the kitchen every now and then and suck a lemon!

October 5th

Rose Hibben was very quiet at lunch today. Somebody finally asked her if she was sad.

"Very," she said.

"Can you tell us why—I mean, besides your age and *tempus fugit*-ing and this gray day?"

"It's silly," Rose answered. "You'll laugh at me."

"Try us."

"All right. I was dusting my apartment this morning, and the old, old soft dust cloth came apart in my hands." She started sniffling. "You see, it was Howard's old

I'm sure I look innocent enough,
sitting in the library looking at a book...."

undershirt...the last one I have. He always told me not to throw out his old 'Skivvie shirts,' as he called them—said they would make great dusters...and they did...And now he's gone...and they're gone...and I'm crying about an old dust rag that had been an undershirt—"

She got up and hurried out, and nobody laughed.

I had a letter from my granddaughter Tricia today, addressed to Hattie McNair, FairAcres Home, Drayton, South Carolina—no Mrs. or Ms., no title at all. Young people these days don't seem to care for titles. My grandson Samuel addressed a note to me last year: Nana McNair. I love the grandchildren calling me Nana, but as a title on an envelope?

Things are getting too casual in the U.S. of A., if you ask me. We're too casual in our dress, our manners, our speech, our mores in general...There's a better word than mores for custom or habit or social usage. Con...con something...

Later

I finally went to the dictionary and went through the cons. Took quite a while, but I rejoiced in finding it: consuetude (kon-swe-tude). I will sleep better now for finding it. A lovely word. Old French. I'd like to use it in a Scrabble game. Fat chance—with ten letters.

October 6th

If I were a Catholic and went to confession, I suppose I'd have to confess that I've become addicted to eavesdropping.

I'm sure I look innocent enough, sitting in the library looking at a book, in a chair by the door to the terrace; but what I'm really doing is listening to a conversation from the terrace, right outside.

Maybe I'm not being fair to Paul and Curtis, but somehow I don't think they'd mind my listening if they knew how many much-needed laughs they have given me. For instance, this evening Curtis said, "My neighbor Jeff and I got to talking one night about dance bands. I said I liked Wayne King's music best.

"Jeff allowed as to how Wayne was all right, but said he wasn't as good as Guylum. So I asked him how he liked Lawrence Welk.

"'I like him, too, but he can't come up to Guylum,' Jeff answered.

"'Who in the world is Guylum?' I asked mystified.

"'You know,' said Jeff, 'the fellow with that band with the sweet horns. Plays on New Year's Eve. Guylum Bardo.'"

Maybe I'll give up eavesdropping for Lent. But I doubt it.

I heard Rose tell someone the other day that she knew a couple who've been married so long they are almost like one person. Rose once heard the man say, "Last night I had such a terrible dream that when I waked up I said to myself..." Bewildered, he turned to his wife, "Honey...what did I say to myself?"

9

—

Devoted Friend

October 8th

I did not put it down in my journal sooner because writing it down would seem to make the awful fact more definite. My friend Sarah Moorer has cancer of the throat, and has known it for several weeks. She is now in the infirmary, for good. She is already having trouble talking, but she managed to tell me that she has refused chemotherapy. I don't blame her. The treatment gives so much discomfort, and any respite it gives would be so temporary in her case.

What do you say to someone in that fix? I was at a terrible loss for words—upset and embarrassed and *so grieved*. Sarah and I have discovered a rapport in recent months that seemed to be a joy for us both. It certainly has been for me. Many people here are as kind and caring as Sarah, but not very many have her brightness of mind and spirit. I taught her to play Scrabble, and we had such fun making outrageous words.

I can't accept what is happening to my dear friend. She is seventy-three, and some people would say, "That's a goodly age. She's had a long life. Let her go!" But I'm not ready to! And I don't believe she's ready to go.

She hasn't had an easy life. She lost her only child...and her husband...and recently her beloved brother, Richard. Not only that, but she had to work hard for her living. In one of our conversations she told me that this last year at FairAcres had given her more rest and ease than she had ever expected to have again. She appreciated being looked after, and not having to cook or clean or go to the grocery or do laundry. She loved our resident nurses and all the staff, enjoyed their attention and care, and she expected to enjoy all of this for several more years.

One thing she has relished here is the time to read. She said the lack of time for reading had always been a frustration. Now, with leisure and a good library, she was reveling in books. We both made lists for future reading.

Another thing we had in common was our dislike of housework. We agreed that there is nothing more boring than dusting the same old furniture and sweeping the same old porch, over and over.

Sarah and I were saving our money toward a dream: a cruise to Alaska (not in the summer; the bargain cruises are in spring and fall). Now of course she will never see the Inside Passage...those glorious icy heights...Sitka and Nome.

What's much worse, she has to face weeks—maybe months—of suffering. Most people with cancer of the throat were heavy smokers, I've heard. Sarah never smoked. I don't believe she's ever done anything really wrong. So why? Why? Why?

I seem to be talking to myself more and more these days. It's getting bad. One day the door to the hall was partly open. Cora rapped on the door and came in, saying, "Are you all right, Hattie? I was passing by going to lunch and heard what sounded like an argument."

"I'm fine," I said. "I was just arguing with myself. I don't know who won," I added, laughing.

October 9th

Tilly Horton said today, "My two youngest grands— Mary's Hilliard and Tom's Anna Lee—are learning to drive. Fifteen years old—just *barely*. Isn't that awful? Somehow I worry more about them driving than I did about my children. Maybe it's because there are more cars on the road these days." After a minute she said, "And maybe it's because I'm older and know better *how* to worry than I used to!"

Our names! Hattie...Louly...Tilly. Lordy!

We got to talking about names the other day. Cora said, "How could my mother saddle me with such an ugly, harsh name as Cora?"

"How about mine?" I chimed in. "I've always resented it. With names out there like Daphne...and Melissa...and Chlotilde...and Jacqueline—I have to be *Hattie*. I could wish my mother hadn't loved her sister Harriet quite so much."

Tilly said, "Anyway, it's not as bad as what the stern Pilgrims used to name their daughters: Faith, Hope, and Charity. Those are all right; rather nice, in fact. But they didn't stop there. They went into other virtues and traits, giving names like Mercy and Pity. I heard of someone back then named Moderation!"

We whooped over that. "Do you suppose they called her 'Mod'?"

"That's not the worst," went on Cora. "When I was working on my genealogy I learned that I had a New England ancestor named 'Obedience'! Honestly! Can you imagine taking a tiny girl baby and laying such a moniker on her? I wonder if they called her 'Obie'...or maybe 'Beedie'!"

October 11th

Sarah has reached the point in her suffering where she has to be sedated most of the time. When I go to see her there's usually little response. Once in a while, on a better day, she knows I'm there and will smile at me, and maybe return the squeeze of my hand. Because of those times I go often. She has no family to come to see her. The nurses are good to her, but she needs to feel at least one familiar hand.

October 13th

The painkillers are wearing out on Sarah. They're giving her the maximum dosage now. I dread the next few weeks.

October 15th

Sarah has developed pneumonia. When I heard it this morning I couldn't help murmuring, "Praise the Lord." Her suffering should be shortened. I'm told that death from pneumonia is not very painful.

But when I went to the infirmary after breakfast and talked to the head nurse, I was appalled to learn that Sarah would probably be given massive shots of penicillin.

"Dr. Fraser will order it when he comes this morning, I'm sure," she said. "Mrs. Moorer has a very high fever."

"He'll have to deal with me first," I replied. The nurse looked at me strangely, and I was surprised myself at how certain I was that I should get involved on behalf of my friend.

When Dr. Fraser came, he and I went round and round.

"We always administer penicillin when the lungs are in this condition, Mrs. McNair," he insisted. "It's routine."

"And keep her alive to prolong her agony? How can you *dare?*"

"We are trained to sustain life in any way possible." He drew himself up. He was fast losing patience with my interference. "Are you a close relative of Mrs. Moorer's?"

"No. She has no close relatives. I'm a devoted friend. I

saw her add a codicil to her Living Will just a few weeks ago. If you read it, you will see that she would not want these shots you're ordering for her."

He frowned, and I hurried on. "Will you at least wait until I can go to the office and get that will from her file?"

"All right," he said grudgingly. "But hurry, please."

I dashed to the main office, explained the situation to a very helpful young woman, and was back in less than fifteen minutes waving the will and pointing to the handwritten postscript:

"If I am on my 'last legs,' if I have a hopeless illness and I develop pneumonia, I do not want to be given penicillin or any such antibiotic." It was signed, "Sarah L. Moorer." Underneath was the date—three months ago.

"There!" I said proudly.

"Wait a minute," said the doctor. "It's not witnessed. The Living Will is witnessed, but not this added provision."

"It's her handwriting!" I protested. "She signed it, for heaven's sake, and dated it. I saw her do it! I was adding the same thing to my will, the same day!"

Dr. Fraser looked at me for about two long minutes. Finally he shrugged. "I don't like this," he said. "I don't like it at all." But he turned away without giving an order to the nurse and went to see another patient.

October 16th

In thinking about Sarah, I remembered some lines from Emily Dickinson:

The heart asks pleasure first,
And then, excuse from pain;
And then, those little anodynes
That deaden suffering;

"And then, to go to sleep;
And then, if it should be
The will of its Inquisitor,
The liberty to die."

That's what I want for my friend: "The liberty to die."

October 18th

Sarah Moorer died quietly this morning. Praise the Lord.

October 20th

Almost everyone at FairAcres came to Sarah's funeral today in our chapel. She had made a lot of friends.

Christine Summers, who has a hauntingly sweet voice, sang the hymn, "Be Still, My Soul." The music, written by Jan Sibelius, is the same beautiful melody as his *Finlandia*. I like especially one line in it: "All now mysterious shall be bright at last."

Chaplain Brewer read comforting words from the Bible. When he read, "In my Father's house are many mansions," my eyes filled with tears. *I hope you are in a fine mansion, my friend, with everything automatic. No housekeeping—or maybe angels to do the work—angels who adore keeping house.*

I can't help feeling a little bit sorry for Chaplain Brewer. He has to conduct so many funerals. I suppose he knew that when he took the job. Death is a fact of life here—an ever present fact. I'm having that brought home to me more pointedly all the time.

I miss Sarah terribly already. I can't bear to walk down D Hall where her room was.

Oh, I almost forgot to put it down. Dr. Fraser came to the funeral! He gave me a strange look. I'd really like to know what he was thinking. Anyway, he came, and I like him better for it.

10

'Dear Old Ruin'

October 23rd

It seems to me that an unconscionable amount of our time in this world is taken up with the mechanics of living, to-ing and fro-ing with the same actions, day in and day out, that don't really get us anywhere, as in: dressing and undressing; eating and eliminating; making up a bed and then messing it up; filing nails and then watching them grow.

Maybe that's a silly thought, brought on by the monotony of daily tasks in old age, with no goal in view but the grave; and I know that the daily doing of the tasks is necessary for an orderly existence. But I long for a change in the routine, or for something that would give the eternally repeated actions more meaning.

E. B. White must have been in somewhat the same mood when he wrote these lines:

"Commuter: One who spends his life
In riding to and from his wife;
A man who shaves, and takes a train,
And then rides home to shave again."

October 24th

Eye doctors are prescribing artificial tears for many of the people here whose eyes are too dry; but I find I don't need them. There is so much sadness, so many poignant memories, that my eyes get a good laving nearly every day, nature's way.

These days I find it harder to watch sad scenes in movies. I used to be able to say, "Hey, it's only a movie!"—but now the tears come. I suppose it's a weakness that goes along with the white hairs. Anything emotional gets to me...I dread losing control.

Many of us are concerned that our "last stop," our beloved retirement center, is fast turning into a nursing home.

The old rule was that you had to be able to walk in, to dress yourself, and to get to the dining room. This rule is being relaxed to an alarming extent.

It distresses us for visitors to come into our lobby and to see pathetic people sprawled in the chairs at times, napping, with mouths hanging open.

As head of the Residents' Council (oh, groan!) I was asked

to talk to our administrator about it. He allowed that there might have been a few mistakes in admission, but said that most of the cases of deterioration had occurred after admission.

Mr. Detwiler pointed out something I had not thought about. He said, "Not only are people living longer; most older people are in better health these days. Therefore, they put off making applications to homes. The average age of our applicants used to be seventy-four, but now it's eighty-two. By the time some folks are actually admitted, they could be eighty-five, and some of them start going to pieces not long after moving in."

The only solution, it seems to me, is for there to be three components: a retirement center for people still alert and active, an intermediate building for those who are semi-invalids and those becoming "flaky," and an infirmary for the really infirm.

We lack the middle facility here, and we probably won't get it. Not enough money, and no more land to build on.

As my hearing begins to fail I get more and more put out with people who do not speak plainly. I was taught to speak so as to be understood—not to mumble with a lazy tongue as if talking to myself. I was taught that it was impolite to make people have to strain to hear you.

Today if you frown or cup your hand behind your ear to let them know you're not understanding, chances are they'll say, "You'd better get a hearing aid."

I want to say, "Enunciate! Speak up!"

October 26th

A night or two ago I was writing here about getting emotional, about crying. Tonight I *bawled,* with good reason.

I had the radio on, tuned to the FM station that employs an announcer who can pronounce, and who has excellent musical taste. He had found an old, old recording that appealed to him: Alma Gluck singing the words that Thomas Moore wrote to an Irish air, many years ago. It was the song that I—sentimental to the core—chose to be sung at our small, home wedding.

> "Believe me, if all those endearing young charms
> Which I gaze on so fondly today
> Were to change by tomorrow and fleet in my arms
> Like fairy gifts fading away,
> Thou wouldst still be adored, as this moment
>   thou art,
> Let thy loveliness fade as it will;
> And around the dear ruin, each wish of my heart
> Would entwine itself verdantly still.
>
> It is not while beauty and youth are thine own
> And thy cheek unprofaned by a tear
> That the fervor and faith of a soul can be known,
> To which time will but make thee more dear!
> No, the heart that has truly loved never forgets
> But as truly loves on to the close;
> As the sunflower turns to her god, when he sets,
> The same look that she turned when he rose!"

Sam had a sweet voice, and he always sang that song to me on our anniversary. I loved it, until he began to chuckle about "the dear ruin." I wasn't crazy about Mr. Moore's metaphor, but Sam got a lot of fun out of calling me his Dear Old Ruin, as he did out of other names he had for me, particularly "The Poor Old Soul."

October 27th

As I went down a hall of the infirmary today, a patient standing in the doorway of her room motioned for me to come in. "I want to tell you something," she said. "I'm gonna tell you something," she said. "I'm gonna tell you something I don't want anybody else to hear."

We went in her room. She stood by the window, looking out.

"Ma'am, what is it you want to tell me?" I asked.

"Tell you?" She turned around. "Tell you what?"

Oh, me.

October 28th

I had a few shopping errands to do in town today, for some of the shut-ins, and on the way home I dropped by Amelia's house. We had tea in her pleasant kitchen, with two of her children doing homework at a side table. It took me back.

She asked me how the "Kampaign for Kudzu Kottage" was coming along. I told her that it had come to a screeching halt with our unfortunate visit to Mr. Andrew Hoskins.

"I told you!" she said. "He's impossible...but it's funny, last night I suddenly remembered something about him that concerns Miss Minna McKenzie."

"Really?"

"Yes. It was something Mama told me. Let's see, now...When Miss Minna had only been teaching piano a year or two, she had a pupil who was about fifteen years old—and quite pudgy. Andrew Hoskins! I know it's hard to think of his being fat—he's so skinny now; but apparently he had a case of adolescent blubber.

"At that time Mama had decided to take a few lessons, to brush up on the piano so she could play while she was stuck at home with babies."

"Oh," I said, "I remember how well Lucy could play when we were at Converse. I was always sorry she didn't major in piano."

"She was good," Amelia nodded. "Still is. Anyway, Miss Minna's pupils were giving a recital for their parents and friends, and just before it came time for Andrew to play, he ran out of the house, and I don't think he ever went back to Miss Minna's!"

"Why? Stage fright?"

"No. He didn't like the name of the piece of music she had picked out for him to play. He thought everybody would laugh when she announced that he, her fattest pupil, would play 'The Elephant Waltz'!"

We had to chuckle over that, and decided we didn't blame him a bit.

October 29th

Today I was on duty in the library, and Miss Minna came in to get a book. I told her about Amelia's memory. She laughed, but she had a chagrined look, too.

"Poor Andrew!" she said. "I played a bad trick on him, without meaning to. I had no idea he was so sensitive about his weight."

"You never can tell about adolescents. What a terrible time of life! Did he ever come back for another lesson?" I asked.

"No, he didn't. I've always regretted that incident, Hattie. I've felt badly about not ever telling him I was sorry."

October 30th

Lying in bed last night I had a brainstorm. Maybe it wasn't too late for Miss Minna to apologize!

This morning I went to visit her and approached her with the idea. I told her about the Kudzu Kottage situation—of the great need to help out a fine young couple and to rescue a dear, small, endangered house at the same time. As I excitedly spilled out my plan, she looked a bit bewildered.

"I don't know, Hattie. So many years have passed—about sixty, in fact."

Even with a troubled look on her face, she was appealing. Her brows and the way her eyes were set had something to do with it. She had kept her good bone structure, and her features hadn't lost their definement as they had with most of us, especially ones who had gained weight.

I had a sudden thought: Maybe Miss Minna looks like she does because she didn't have a husband and children to beat her down...Immediately I was sorry for that thought. *Forgive me, dear ones.*

"Better late than never, Miss Minna," I encouraged. "You could tell him that you'd been doing some reviewing of your life—all of us do, at this stage—and that you remembered the incident and wanted to tell him you were sorry. If he has an ounce of decency left—"

"Oh, I'm sure he does. He was a nice boy." she said.

"And then you could gently work the talk around to the cottage. You could tell him that when you saw its condition— I'll take you to see it this afternoon—it distressed you. Miss Minna, nobody in the world would want to distress you!"

She looked uncertain, but she smiled, "And I don't want to distress *you*, Hattie. You're very persuasive."

It was decided that not only would we go to see the little house this afternoon, but also I would drive her to see Mr. Hoskins.

We set out after lunch, first to the nearby cottage. It was shocking to see how the kudzu had reclaimed places we had worked so hard to clear. We didn't get out of the car, but Miss Minna shook her head sadly at the forlorn look of the empty bungalow and the unkempt yard.

On the way into town we agreed again that it would be

best if I not go in with her. When we reached the square, I parked and showed her the entrance to the second-floor office. She was uncertain about climbing the steep steps, however, so we determined that we would drive to Mr. Hoskins's home and keep trying until we caught him there.

We were lucky enough to catch him there on the first try.

As I watched from the car in the driveway, she made her way carefully to the front door and rang the bell. I saw the door open narrowly and then more widely. All I saw of Mr. Hoskins was a hand extended to guide Miss Minna through the door, which then closed behind her.

As I waited, I tried to read the magazine I had brought, but without much success. *Dear Lord, please don't let him talk roughly to that dear soul.* I had qualms. Was I turning into a full-time busybody?

Thirty minutes passed. I felt better. He had thrown Christine and me out in five.

About ten minutes later, I heard voices. He was helping her down the steps. They were both smiling! My heart rejoiced.

He opened the car door for her but paid no attention to whoever was driving. As my passenger buckled up, I backed out carefully and eased the car up Oleander Street. Miss Minna waved, but Andrew Hoskins had already disappeared.

"Hattie, you're a wizard!" she said, turning to me. "I'm *so* glad I talked to him. Poor Andrew! He's so lonely...He showed me an album filled with nothing but pictures he had taken of Annie—some of her garden, with their longtime pet dog; some at the beach. Annie was his whole life."

"Did you…were you able to suggest—?"

"About the cottage? Yes, yes, I got it in! He said he would think about it—and would consider renting it."

"To the Priests?"

"I think so. I believe the thing now would be to have Arthur go to see him."

I never did learn exactly what had transpired. I only know that whereas Chris and I had struck out completely, Miss Minna had hit a home run. I tried to figure it out. Was it her soft voice? Her sweet smile? Probably…combined with the fact that she was part of his past.

Here was a sweet face from his youth. Here she was, apologizing, asking him to forgive her. I suppose no heart in the world would be hard enough to resist her.

Praise the Lord! Maybe there's room in this cruel world for some busybodies after all.

October 31st

Arthur has already been to see Mr. Hoskins!

"That's one difficult old man," Arthur said after the conversation. "I can't understand how he can let a place go to the dogs, and then when he finally decides to rent it, he gets hard as nails."

"I guess he's returning to the old days in his business," I said, "when he made a lot of money by being hard. Don't let it worry you too much. I'm sure you'll manage to please him."

"I'll try. Lord knows, I'll try. We're gonna make that place

He was helping her down the steps. They were both smiling!

shine. What bothers me is, how can I ever thank you and Miss Minna and Mrs. Summers and the two gentlemen?"

"Don't worry about that either," I patted his arm. "We'll take pleasure in seeing you and Dollie and the boys get nicely settled—and the baby when she, or he, comes. By the way, how is Dollie? And will you be able to get some things for a nursery? You don't really have enough furniture for the house, do you?"

"No'm, we don't, but Dollie's doin' just fine," he said, with his pleasant smile. Then he continued somewhat tentatively, "We'll make do, and we'll be all right. Maybe we can get a piece or two of furniture secondhand. The main thing is, we'll have some room. Oh, Lord! How good it's gonna be to spread out!"

Arthur could have whined and complained pitifully about the things he doesn't have, but that wasn't his way. He was joyous and appreciative of what we had done for him. So— there is activity again among my busybody genes. We must get some money some way, to buy furniture for Kudzu Kottage!

Our food is served cafeteria style, so we have to line up to get it, and sometimes the line is painfully long. There's a bench where we can sit (in line), and on a wall near the bench is a menu list, which we can read (forty times!) while we wait.

One day recently I was pleased to see that we were going to get quiche for lunch; but a man down the line was skeptical.

"What in the world is 'quickie'?" he asked.

11

Celebrations

November 1st

I had an interesting invitation recently from Tennessee, to attend the celebration of an old friend's "seventeenth quinquennium." That sent me running to the dictionary. I learned that a quinquennium is a term of five years, so, with pencil and paper, I figured that my friend George's years had reached a total of eighty-five—a goodly number, especially for a man.

My husband and I used to talk and wonder about the fact that women outlive their spouses in most cases. At least *I* wondered. Sam said there was no mystery about it—that men die earlier because they work harder and have more stress. Well, maybe that was true, some years ago; but nowadays many, many women have jobs that are as hard as men's, and they have child care to boot.

Do women have heartier genes? Do we take better care of our hearts and lungs? Fewer women than men are heavy smokers, it seems to me.

I believe a lot of girls of my generation were turned on to smoking by the glamorous ads. Remember "Blow Some My Way!"? I think that was the one with a gorgeous couple in a snazzy convertible, top down, climbing a hill in the moonlight.

Then there was the ad that said, "Reach for a Lucky Instead of a Sweet," with a lovely svelte girl pictured. Oh, boy! Did that cause a ruckus! The candy companies raised Cain. I think they got the ad banned.

A wonderful treat last night on FM radio: Henry Mancini and James Galway playing "Seventy-Six Trombones" on two flutes. Marvelous!

November 2nd

Tonight after supper some of us sat around downstairs talking about things we wished we had done in our lives. I said I'd always wished for the nerve to pilot a hang glider—to take off from a mountain and float over a valley. It always looks like smooth, easy sailing—gently soaring. Lovely.

Edwin said, "That's not for me. Too many of 'em have crashed...I wish I'd gone up in a balloon though, and drifted over a spectacular scene like...the Alps, or Lake Como...or, let me see..."

"The Appalachian Mountains in the fall?" someone suggested.

"Right. Or the Irish countryside, green and rolling. Just drifted slowly and peacefully, over all those cows and sheep—"

"I wish I'd ridden in a submarine, and submerged," chimed in Curtis.

"Not really! Not in one of those tight, closed-in things!" someone else protested.

Tilly said she wished she could have ice-skated, or skied. (Is that the right way to put the past tense on ski?) Those were two sports denied us in the South, until recently.

I said that I wish I had learned to play "Lo, Hear the Gentle Lark" on a silver flute, and Lucius started nodding his head.

"I know what you mean," he said. "I wish I had learned to play the xylophone."

"Honestly?" I asked. "That surprises me. You'd really like to hit those tinkly pieces of metal with two little hammers?"

"Yep," he said. "Either that, or play the tuba—oompah, oompah!"

We all laughed. What contrasting ambitions!

Tilly came to my apartment after the wishing session. We had a glass of wine and put our feet up.

"That was fun," said Tilly, "telling what we wish we'd done...Of course, I couldn't tell them what I wish, more than anything, that I'd done."

"Can you tell me?" I asked.

"Maybe so." She looked into her wine glass, sadly. "Hattie, I

wish I had been more appreciative of Russell—of my husband.
The sweetest man...I know now that his good heart was
worth more than anything—but I didn't think so then. I
wanted a bigger house, a better car. I wanted to be the wife of
the president of the Rotary Club, or the wife of the mayor, or
the senator. I thought I would be better in those positions than
any of the women who had them."

I had never known Russell—had not known Tilly Horton
until recently. I didn't know what to say, so I took a sip of
wine. Tilly got up and went to the window and looked out.
Her face was as bleak as the sky.

"All the time I had this dear man—loving and helpful and
funny—and I didn't know what I had until he was dead. I
remember how surprised I was at the great number of people
who came to his funeral. They knew him better than I did! I
don't think I ever once let him know that I valued his
sweetness...Oh, dear God! If I could just have him here, right
now, for five minutes! I don't know what I'd do—but he'd find
out how I feel *now*...Oh, Hattie, I was such a fool!"

She started to cry, and before I could even try to console
her, she ran out of the room. I felt desolated. How much
grief we suffer when we start regretting, and lamenting.

"With rue my heart is laden." That was Housman, I
think. And somebody else—???—said:

> "We look before and after
> And pine for what is not."

Oh, me.

Ruminating later

Women in their upper thirties are talking a lot these days about the ticking of their biological clocks.

Those of us who have put a great deal more mileage on our pedometers do a lot of thinking (if not talking) about our mortal clocks, and their inevitable ticking.

We know that the countdown is continuing—four... three...two. "The days grow short when you reach September." November looms. "These precious days I'd spend with you," but the "you" in your life is so often not there anymore. His mortal clock ran down, so instead of tandem—lovely tandem—you have to finish the race as a lonely solo runner.

Trite, fatuous thoughts for rainy days, especially cold November days.

We all laughed recently about the man who said he felt so old he didn't even dare to buy a green banana. I used to subscribe to the Charleston paper for a year at a time. Now I subscribe for six months, and am thinking of changing to three months next time!

Somebody—some comedian—said, "I'm not afraid of dying; I just don't want to be around when it happens."

But happen it will—and at that moment it will be a one-woman show—no backup crew, no fellow players—a solo performance. There will probably be an audience, alas: my children. I'm almost sure I will want them around me, and yet...Suppose, in spite of my faith, my courage fails me at the last, and I go out whimpering?

I like Negro spirituals. There's one so plaintive in its melody and words that it always gives me pause.

"You gotta go to that lonesome valley.
You gotta go there by yourself.
Ain't no one to go there with you.
You gotta go there by yourself."

Geneva Tinken has been talking a lot about death lately. The other day she was sitting in the lobby, immersed in her large-print Bible. I stopped to speak to her, but she waved me off: "Can't stop to chat now, Hattie. I'm crammin' for my finals."

Oh, me. I think tomorrow I'll go to the Country Store and get something wicked. Not something made of yogurt and saccharin. I want real cream and sugar and nuts and chocolate. A double dip!

Later

I can't seem to get death off my mind. I recall some lines from "Thanatopsis," by William Cullen Bryant, that impressed me muchly when I was a teenager:

"…sustained and soothed
by an unfaltering trust, approach thy grave
Like one who wraps the draperies of his couch
About him, and lies down to pleasant dreams."

When I first read Bryant's exhortation I thought it nobly

poetic advice. At that time, death was so far down the road
that it was an insubstantial idea, a phantasm. I believe I
actually thought it never would really happen to me!

Now that the insubstantial gains more substance every
day, I am trying to develop a peaceful frame of mind.
Maybe I should practice wrapping the "draperies" (!) of my
"couch" about me, in a soothing, confident way

(Of course, Dear Diary, I know that the main thrust of
the poem comes sooner, in the line that states, "So live,
that when thy summons comes." But it's a little late to
think about *that* angle.)

November 3rd

Arthur and Dollie have moved! Mr. Hoskins broke down
and said they could start their tenancy. The lease is for one
year only, but I don't worry about that. Arthur will
improve that place until the old man will beg him to stay
on. Arthur says he has hopes that Mr. Hoskins will agree to
sell the house to him, in a few years.

Those two young people have done a typically nice thing.
They've asked everybody at the Home to come over
Saturday afternoon to a housewarming! I will pray for a
warm day.

November 5th

Today *was* a lovely, warm day, thank goodness. A number
of us walked, and the FairAcres' bus made two trips this
afternoon to Kudzu Kottage. (I still call it that, although

the vicious vine has been completely removed now from the house itself—thanks to the fall weather and to Arthur's coworkers who organized a massive cleanup of that pest.)

The maintenance department had taken over several long folding tables and folding chairs today and set them up under the pines and live oaks, and Dollie and her mother had loaded the tables with good, country cooking.

I heard Dollie say, when someone thanked her for a home-fried doughnut and a cup of cider, "Oh, we feel like you all at the Home are our folks! And we sure do appreciate what some of you have done for us...Go in and look at the house. It's kind of empty, but it's clean. We just love it. Arthur wants to paint the outside...pretty soon."

I knew she meant, "When we can save enough money for the paint." And I know he'll get it somehow, and with his careful work, fresh white paint will bring out the gingerbread trim and the unique banisters.

Arthur assisted some of us up the steps, and he was grinning from ear to ear. The way he looked at the ones of us who had helped him made it all worthwhile.

The two little boys, Artie and Cliff, were almost overcome by all the excitement. They were charmingly shy, which suited us just fine. This generation is surfeited with brassy, loud, know-it-all children.

The house had been scrubbed and polished to a fare-thee-well—but oh, the bareness of it! Young Artie, aged four, took me by the hand and led me around. "We've got *six rooms!*" he said, proudly. "Six *big* rooms!"

The living room had nothing but a fern in it, on the floor by a window, and two chairs. The dining room was completely bare. One bedroom held only an ironing board. In the kitchen there were a card table and four chairs. Fortunately there are some nice built-in cabinets in the kitchen, in pretty good shape.

November 6th

Christine, Louly, Lucius, Sidney, and I held a called "executive" meeting tonight after supper. We named ourselves the Kudzu Kottage Kommittee and declared the urgent item of the day to be: furniture.

November 7th

Today we solicited ideas for making some money. Gusta said, "I love yard sales. Let's have a humongous one!"

That notion was voted down, reluctantly. We don't have enough junk—or even "junque." We gave it all away before moving here.

Someone thought of a lottery, but we decided that might not sit too well with the administration.

I think it was Sidney who came up with the idea of having an "Evening of Recollections" to raise money. That will give all of us a chance to dig into our memories for funny or poignant events that we would be willing to share. Since this is Memory Alley here, it ought to be an interesting and entertaining evening.

It was suggested to hold the event close to Christmas and

make it part of the season of "holiday giving," especially
since it is for such a worthwhile cause. We discussed
whether to charge admission or just to take up a collection
after warming everyone up with some thigh-slapping
stories. I think most of us favor the latter approach.

Speaking of "junk" and of "Christmas," the holiday
deluge has begun. I lugged a heavy pile of no-account mail
to my apartment from our post office today: catalogs from
New England for cold-weather garb I'll never need here in
Dixie, a catalog from Ireland for crystal I have no use for, a
flyer for wigs (well, maybe, some day soon, alas), a catalog
from Hammacher-Schlemmer for gadgets I have no room
for, and on and on. I hate to think of how many trees it
takes to make the paper for all those pieces of wasted
solicitation.

At least today I worked a rhyme out of the situation:

JUNK MAIL
Mailing lists are odious things.
I seem to be on several.
I don't know how my name got on
And get it off, I never'll.

I kind of like that "never'll." It has a teeny-tiny sound of
Ogden Nash. Oh, that man—my idol. I felt bereft when he
died. I wrote some lines about him—completely inade-
quate, but the best I could do:

UPON THE DEATH OF OGDEN NASH
He's gone, and the world of wit is diminished
But his account will not be finished
As long as we quote from his "Belle of Old
    Natchez"
(The girl who said, "When I itches I scratchez").
Who else would take a kitchen faucet
And rhyme it with a woman's caucet?
Or write about the lowly soy-bean
(He couldn't tell a girl- from a boy-bean).
He wouldn't like a sad farewelling
But, oh! We'll miss his fractured spelling!
May he find fresh fields of rhyme and meter
To gladden the heart of good Saint Peter!

12

Ruminations

November 9th

Somehow or other we got on the subject of highways today at the dinner table. I said that I suppose sleek, fast interstates are necessary, but they're oh, so monotonous.

Ethel said, "You're right. You have to sing *loud*, to keep awake." She went on to say that she feels sorry for traveling children these days. Passing no farms, they can't see a pony or a pig or a windmill. They can't play cow poker.

Dr. Browning said, "I miss legends, such as 'Leaving Andalusia County. Entering Dinwiddie County.'" (Oh, the sounds of American names. Wonderful!) "And signs like: 'Near this spot General So-and-so's forces surprised the British forces under General So-and-so.'"

"I even miss the signs that just said THINK," Louly commented. "Who put those up, anyway?"

Nobody knew.

We all agreed that half the fun of getting there used to be reading—aloud—the Burma Shave ads. Curtis remembered one: "In this world of toil and sin, your head grows bald but not your chin!"

We all deplored today's unimaginative signs, which read "Rest Area Ahead." "Gas and Food This Exit." Or, "Do Not Park on the Median." No rhythm. No color. "Slow. Toll Gate Ahead." (At least there's a nice little sign that comes on after you've dropped your money that says "Thank You.")

Curtis said, "Once in a while there's a right interesting exit sign for towns, like one in North Carolina for 'Apex, Fuquay- Varina.'"

Somebody else remembered intriguing sounding destinations in Virginia, "Exit: Ladysmith and Culpeper," and "Exit: Manassas and Dumfries."

In his dry way, Dr. Browning commented, "There's a road sign in South Carolina that points to Clinton in one direction and to Prosperity in the opposite direction…Do you suppose that should tell us something?"

November 12th

Ben Croft, a beloved retired minister in my hometown, is frequently called on to conduct funerals, particularly by people who want a eulogy. He is a eulogizer from way back.

He digs and finds things to admire about the dear departed and leaves the family all aglow with pride and fond memories.

I ran into a friend from home recently who said to me, "I'm so afraid Ben will die before he gets to conduct my funeral! His health is not good at all. He's the only one who could make my children think their Mama was somebody!"

She looked thoughtful for a minute and then added, "Hattie, you know what? I think I'll get Ben to do my eulogy and put it on a tape!"

It happened! I'll swear.

November 15th

A laugh for today:
Edwin told this at the table. He said President Clinton was visiting an old folks' home. He sat down beside a nice-looking old lady and talked to her about the weather and her health, etc. After a few minutes, he asked her, "Ma'am, do you know who I am?"

She shook her head, patted him on the hand, and said sweetly, "No, dear. I'm sorry I don't. But if you go over there to the desk, they'll tell you who you are."

I don't like having people call our country's president "Bill." Nor did I like "Jimmy" a few years ago. The office deserves a more dignified moniker. I like Rutherford and Theodore, Warren and Woodrow—and even Franklin.

Calvin Coolidge was sometimes referred to as "Cal"—but not to his face!

Tilly told us a funny story today about her grandson, aged six. His older sister had just had her tonsils removed and had received much attention and many gifts. The boy began to clear his throat and cough and put his hands to his throat whenever his parents were near. Finally, not getting the desired response, he went up to his mother and said, "Mama, I think you'd better take me to the hospital quick. My tonsils are loose!"

November 19th

One of our residents, Hector McDill, had his driver's license taken away yesterday. What a hullabaloo!

He went to the police station and raised a ruckus. His wife, Ethel (several years his junior), said the talk went something like this:

"Whadda you mean, lifting my license? I've been driving since before you were born!"

"Yes, sir. We know that. It says here that you're ninety-one years old."

"And what's wrong with that?"

"Well, sir, apparently you're not seeing too well. You turned left on a red light on Main Street, and three blocks later you did it again!"

"Well, that's not anything so terrible. They don't make those lights bright enough, anyhow. When the sun's shining on 'em you can't tell if they're pink or purple or pea green...I'm gonna write the guv'nor about this. You'll be hearing from him. He won't hold with removin' a man's transportation just for some little ol' infraction—Excuse me, ma'am.... Oh, it's you, Ethel."

She said Hector had been sputtering and muttering ever since. Said nothing had upset him so much since George Bush lost the election to "that spike-haired upstart from Arkansas with the pants-wearin' wife."

It *is* a traumatic thing to be removed from that position behind a wheel where you've spent much of your life—in control. I suppose it's worse for a man. Removes part of his "macho."

Maybe there ought to be an arbitrary age for people to stop driving—say eighty-five. Then we'd all know ahead; there'd be no embarrassment. That might be better than the chance we take of having those valuable little cards, with the ugly photographs, removed forcibly and unexpectedly from our wallets one day.

We were also talking at the table today about nicknames. I told them about a woman in my hometown who was called by a rather strange name. It sounded like "Cooter" or "Cudda."

I asked a friend of hers how she got the name, and how it really should be pronounced.

"It's 'Could-a,'" said the acquaintance. "She's a real bridge-playing fool. Plays a good game and knows it. She's always saying, 'You could-a bid three hearts,' or 'You could-a led a spade.' She said it so much, we stuck it on her!"

Southern people do love nicknames.

December 1st

When I moved to FairAcres, I brought one box of notebooks and scrapbooks—my life, condensed to fit in a Campbell's Soup carton that could go under a bed.

I've been going through the notebooks thinking about our Recollections Night that is planned now for December 15th (close enough to Christmas, we hope, to catch people in a generous spirit). Some of the words sound strangely unfamiliar. Did I write that? I wonder sometimes. It's my handwriting...

I found a few notes I put down on a trip Sam and I took to the Midwest one summer in the early 1960s. He had to go on business, and since the children were away at summer school or camp, I was glad to go along to a part of the country I'd never seen. Here are some of my jottings:

> Few road signs marred the pretty rolling scenery in Kentucky and Indiana. Occasionally on the side of a barn we'd see the words, "Chew Mail Pouch Tobacco." There weren't even any of the Clabber Girl Baking Powder or Tube Rose Snuff signs that we saw in parts of western North Carolina.
>
> On the car radio today, from some station in Ohio, we heard so-called religious songs, sung

nasally and endlessly. The announcer said at one point, "We'll now hear from the en-tar quar." He announced an upcoming Holy Ghost Festival. Then a man sang about the Promised Land. One line *killed* me: "I'll shake hands with my mother, over thar."

...This afternoon we drove through corn country, corn "as high as an elephant's eye," miles and miles of it, with tremendous ears on every stalk. We wondered how there could be any hunger in the world. Many a Post-Toastie there.

I also found some notes that reminded me of how bored Sam and I used to get while helping our children with their reading homework. Those primers were so utterly inane. "Oh, see Dick. See Dick run. Oh, see Spot. See Spot jump."

I remember one morning when Sam went to wake up John, our second-grader. Instead of just telling him to get up, Sam said, slowly and deliberately, "Run to the john, John. Run, John, run."

Sam's wonderful sense of humor smoothed out many a rough spot on our journey.

In one notebook I kept some quotes I've liked especially (and obviously gathered from all over at random).

"Better is a dry morsel and quietness therewith than an house full of sacrifices with strife."
—Proverbs 17:1

"Better than old beef is tender veal. I want no
woman thirty years of age."
—Chaucer in *The Canterbury Tales* (the old goat!)

"I like a Highland friend who will stand by me, not
only when I am in the right, but when I am a little in
the wrong!"
—Sir Walter Scott

"Put your trust in God, but keep your powder dry."
—Oliver Cromwell

"Conscience is the fear that someone will see you."
—H. L. Mencken

"Get thy tools ready. God will find the work."
—Robert Browning

I've also found many examples of my lifelong penchant
for rhyme-making. I wonder if anybody anywhere (besides
me) remembers a fellow named Colonel Stoopnagle and his
odd way with language. His foolish spelling intrigued me,
to the point of writing this—many, many years ago:

STOOPNAGLE ENGLISH
To your Colonelship, A.B., cum lowdy,
Greetings and a friendly haude.
I like your style, but, entre noo,

Aren't some things just a bit tous tous?
Uncle Sam's English is hard enuff
Without a lot of funny stough.
Before you reach the pearly gaight*
Shouldn't you, once, spell something strate?
(*Are my directions mixed, my Kernel?
P'raps you expect the fires infolonel.)

December 5th

Yesterday I went to Miss Minna's room to talk about ordering some two-piano numbers. Last week we persuaded Mr. Detwiler to move a spinet piano from the lobby into the large parlor, near the Steinway, so that we can really "go to town" on selections arranged for four hands *on two pianos!* Fortunately, right now the two instruments are in tune.

Miss Minna went to her closet to get a music company's catalog from a shelf, and I, idly, picked up a small leather-bound book of poetry from a table by my chair. I was intrigued by the small, beautiful piece of heavy silk marking her place.

The book fell open to that place, and the poem on that page was "Ann Rutledge" by Edgar Lee Masters. I was reading it when I heard, "Oh, *please! No!*" from Miss Minna.

As I looked up, startled by the distress in her voice, I saw an equally distressed look on her face. She took the book from me, settled the marker very carefully, and placed the book on her bedside table. I was too surprised to say anything. She mumbled an apology, and we went on with our search for duo-piano selections; but I could not forget the intensity of her reaction.

No one except the owner was supposed to handle that little book, or move the marker. She probably kept the book out of sight most of the time, and had just happened to be reading it when I came unexpectedly.

Tonight I got out all my collections of poetry, and in one of them I found "Ann Rutledge," from Masters's *Spoon River Anthology*. I remembered seeing, in Miss Minna's book, penciled markings around three or four lines in the middle of the poem. She hadn't given me time to read them, but now I knew they were these lines:

> "I am Ann Rutledge, who sleeps beneath these
> weeds,
> Beloved in life of Abraham Lincoln;
> Wedded to him, not through union,
> But through separation."

And I knew—I positively knew—that Miss Minna's one and only love, Grainger Pendarvis, had sent her that book, had marked the page with white silk ribbon, and had marked the lines with his own hand.

She wanted no other eyes to see the poem, no other hands to move the marker he had placed. I didn't blame her. His action had told her so much. She cherished it. Who could blame her?

I don't need to put any artificial tears in my eyes tonight. My own salty ones have flowed freely.

December 7th

I have a terrible time remembering names these days. There are so many people in this place, so many names. When I go to introduce two people to each other, I'm embarrassed. The minute I know I have to call up a name, it runs away, and I'm left stuttering: "I want you to meet...uh...this is a friend of mine...uh..."

One of life's low moments. And I'm finding lately that it's not only names of people that elude me, but names of ordinary things I've known intimately, all my life.

The other day I went into a drug store (not the corner drug store, but the large, discount variety) to get some Band-Aids. Usually you serve yourself in that store, but a young man in a white jacket came toward me. I suppose he thought that the Poor Old Soul looked like she could use some assistance.

"Ma'am, may I help you?" he asked politely.

"Yes, thank you. I want some—" Oh, dear. The words "Band-Aids" had taken a nosedive into some deep scuttle of my mind, and I could not pull them out.

The young man kept looking at me, so finally I said, "I want some little strips." I measured two or three inches with my fingers.

"Ma'am, what kind of little strips?"

"Well, let's see...they have adhesive on them."

He went away and came back with a roll of adhesive tape.

I shook my head. He shrugged his shoulders. I made one more effort.

"They come in a little tin box."

"Oh-h-h!" he said, a light dawning. "You mean *Band-Aids!*"

I soon left with my package, and with the fervent hope that I would never see that young man again.

That afternoon, as so often happens lately, the neurons and synapses in my poor brain were not connecting. I think there are lapses in my synapses!

A little girl named Betty, aged four, was visiting her grandmother here recently. At bedtime Grandma heard her prayers, but after the Amen the dear child added a postscript: "And God, please make all these old people new!"

Needless to say, that little girl could win a popularity contest on our campus any day.

I heard about another little girl recently who is a true Daughter of the Confederacy. She named her Easter bunny "Rabbit E. Lee!"

December 8th

I've been reading this journal, and it seems there's a preponderance of stories that are jokes, stories that make monkeys out of some of the residents. I suppose that's because I like to laugh and to make others laugh; but I'm depressed now because I feel that I'm not painting a true picture of this Home.

It's easier to describe the "Nuts" and their nuttiness than to delineate the goodness and kindness that occurs here all day, every day; but I should not simply omit that facet of our life. There is much courage and selflessness displayed.

For instance: There are people among us who will get up at dawn to drive a fellow "inmate" to the hospital for an eight o'clock CAT scan or X ray or whatever, and stay until it is done. And these drivers are often people in their eighties who could be spending their "golden years" in a rocking chair, saying, "To heck with other people's troubles. I have enough of my own."

There are many folks who spend hours trying to cheer up people in the infirmary. Sometimes on pretty days they push various ones out into the sun, in wheelchairs, or take them to walk. (Sometimes you wonder a little who's leaning on whom.)

Some of the patients are from rather far away, and have no relatives nearby. So our good angels find out what they need and go shopping. They also get up games and sing-alongs.

My hat is off to them. I wish I had their patience and goodness. At least I can write a line about them once in a while, herein. Q.E.D.

13

Recollections

December 10th

Sidney has us all recollecting. I turned my mind back, all the way to early childhood, and came up with some memories that I cherish. I probably won't tell them on Recollections Night next week; these are not that entertaining. But I want to put them down here. Maybe one of my children will be glad to read them some day.

As a child I spent several weeks every summer at my grandparents' home in Alabama. This was pretty close to heaven for a city-bred youngster. The house was on a three-acre lot on the edge of a small, sleepy town. There were two horses, a cow, chickens, and pigs. But best of all there was Colie.

Colie at fifteen was as big as a man, good-natured, and

Sidney has us all recollecting.

very black. In the winter he did chores around the place after school, mostly cutting and hauling wood for the fireplaces. In the summer his main occupation seemed to be to keep the visiting grandchildren occupied and happy, and this he did joyfully.

He could make games out of nothing. With some tin cans and string he rigged up a "telephone" line that ran from the window of an upstairs bedroom to the buggy shed. I would sit in the window and order groceries.

"No ma'am, Miss Hattie, we ain't got no mush melons today. We's fresh out. But we got some larrupin' good cowpeas"

He made slots in an old crate for post office boxes. With some old letters stolen from my uncle's desk (he was a bachelor, and some of them were love letters), we rigged up a post office. I was post mistress, of course.

Colie would come sidling up to the window and say, "Any mail t'day for Mister Mawkinbird?" I usually found some mail for Mr. Mockingbird and for my brother and cousins—an old catalog, or a perfumed love letter.

Usually Colie kept us out of trouble; but one day he was polishing my uncle's shoes and didn't notice that my cousins, Thad and Peter, were fooling around with the ropes in the well. The cook had hung a bucket of buttermilk in the well to keep cool. The two boys managed to tip it over and ruined all the water in the well!

Colie was called on the carpet, and we all felt worse about that than about the well having to be drained.

One day my brother said, "Colie, what are you going to do when you grow up?"

Colie thought a minute, grinned, and said, "I'm gonna git married, and set down!"

One summer the cousins had gone home, and only my brother, John, then aged about eight, and I, only about five, were left. Mama and Grandma were invited to a tea at a house down the street and wanted to go, but they were afraid to leave Grandpa unattended. He had hardening of the arteries and was "not quite himself," as the euphemism went. (He was really barmy, in a gentle way.) The cook and Colie had finished their work and gone home.

John said, "We'll stay with him, Grandma. We'll take good care of him." Finally it was decided that they would go to the party for a short while.

They had only been gone a few minutes when Grandpa said, "Children, I think I will go up town. I have some business to attend to."

We were big-eyed with astonishment and fear. He was not allowed out alone. It was a pathetic case: a tall, bearded, soft-spoken Southern gentleman, a respected lawyer who had served in the United States Congress, now trying to persuade two small children to "let him out."

While he was mumbling about who he had to see "up town," John slipped out of the room. "Watch him," John whispered to me as he went by. "I'll be right back."

I kept my eyes glued on the poor old fellow, who was straightening his tie and patting down his hair. "Now I must find my hat," he said. He went to the rack in the hall to get his Panama, but it was not there. Then it dawned on me: John had hidden it!

Grandpa searched in every closet in the house.

"Little daughter," he said to me more than once, "can't you *please* help me find my hat?"

I made a pretense of looking, and so did John. He winked at me, and I knew what he meant. Grandpa, in his great dignity, would not think of stepping out of the house with his head uncovered.

I forget now where the hiding place was—behind the stove in the kitchen, maybe. Anyway, we kept the dear old gentleman at home, safe. And I decided what I had long suspected to be true: that my brother, John, was the smartest, brightest creature in the whole wide world. I adored him.

December 12th

I suppose it's hard to wean an American woman away from supermarkets altogether. I thought my grocery shopping days were over when I moved here, but I find myself heading for the Piggly Wiggly every now and then for snacks, Cokes, ice cream, etc.

It's kind of nice—like being back on the old stomping ground, like playing house, without having to haul out heavy loads of cleaning products, potatoes, and meats, and to shop without a newspaper ad in hand or a "green stamp" book.

I have found one thing that is universal about supermarkets: most of the grocery carts have seen better days. Even in our fairly new "Pig" some of the carts squeak and balk and act up. After wrestling with one the other day, I came home and sat down and penned some deathless lines on this very serious subject:

CONTRARINESS
Four lines of empty grocery carts
    And I can't pry one loose!
I pull and jerk and kick and hit,
    Feeling like a goose.

They're welded tight together.
    If at last I get one free
It has one wheel that's headed north
    While the others disagree.

As it bumps along, ker-plunk, ker-plunk
    And squeakily complains,
Somehow I feel a kinship
    With the aging critter's pains!

December 15th

Tonight was Recollections Night, and I was delighted with the turnout in the dining room. All the mobile residents were there, and a number in wheelchairs. There was a festive air, especially with the pretty holiday decorations and table centerpieces already in place.

The maintenance department had installed the movable stage that was kept for such occasions, and the housekeeper had decorated it with lovely greenery and red bows.

Chaplain Brewer opened the festivities, reminding us why we were there, and making a very appropriate prayer. We had asked him to be the master of ceremonies, so he introduced Marcia Coleman as the first "rememberer."

"A lot of my early memories are of relatives visiting us, and talking at the table," Marcia began. "Did any of you all have to put up with that?"

A number of heads nodded, and there were even some claps.

"Well, then, you remember how it was. We wriggled and chafed and sent imploring glances toward our mother, who shook her head. Of course, now I expect we are grateful for the stories we learned then. And occasionally we were rewarded with a rare one like one I remember hearing Uncle Isham Hutchinson tell.

"He said the members of his church, out in the country, had decided one time years ago to do the church over from stem to stern—He didn't say it exactly that way. I suppose it would sound somehow undignified to speak of a church's 'stern.'

"Anyway, Uncle Isham said that at a congregational meeting to decide about some details of the renovation, a lady got up and suggested that the plans should include a large chandelier; whereupon an old recluse named Jonathan Davis stood up and objected. He said that a large chandelier (he pronounced the 'ch' as in 'chicken') would cost too much. 'And besides,' he said 'there's nobody here that could play it!'"

That got a big laugh, and Marcia came down from the stage amid a gratifying round of applause.

Next, Chaplain Brewer introduced Curtis, much to my surprise. He's a pretty quiet fellow as a rule. (Because of my eavesdropping, I know him better than most people here!)

Curtis told us that he had been a disappointment to his mother. "I was her only chick, and she wanted me to shine," he said.

"I wasn't much of a shiner; but I finally got my chance when graduation was coming up—graduation from seventh grade, from our grammar school, that is. There was to be a recitation contest, and Mama was determined for me to take part. She taught me to recite 'Casey at the Bat.' Remember that?" There was a murmur of recognition throughout the audience.

"Lord, how she worked on me! Even took me into the backyard and made me shout those verses all the way across. I got so sick of that poem; but I wanted to please her, so I worked hard.

"On 'the night,' Mama sat in the third row, and I think I kept my eyes on her the whole time. I put everything I had into that piece, and I've never forgotten it. If you'd like to hear it, I'd be pleased to recite for you tonight the only poem I believe I've ever committed to memory."

We let him know that we certainly did want to hear it, and old Curtis once again gave it his all. The audience got right in the spirit of things, and you'd have thought we were at the ball park! *"Stee-rike One!"* he'd shout, and we'd yell and groan.

When he got to the end: "There is no joy in Mudville. Mighty Casey has struck out!" he shook his head sadly, and we clapped 'til our hands hurt.

We weren't surprised when he told us that he had taken first place. He shone! He and his mama won out.

We had decided to take up the collection in the middle of the program, before some of the real oldies got tired and left. This seemed a perfect time, so Sidney—a man who is respected by everybody at FairAcres—got up and said a few words about our "designated receiver."

"I don't have to tell you all anything about Arthur Priest," he said. "I dare say he has mended something or hung up something or cleaned something for everybody in this room, and done it cheerfully and carefully. He's a fine young man, with a fine family, and they need our help. Let's give it to them generously."

We had had the spinet rolled into the dining room and arranged for Miss Minna to play an "offertory." While she played Chopin's Waltz in C-sharp Minor, Lucius and Sidney passed collection plates. As the bills began to pile up, I looked over at Christine and Louly. They grinned at me,

and I grinned at them. I knew what we were all thinking: a
sofa for the living room...a table for the dining room...

Bill Nixon came on next.

"Mine is just a mini-memory," he said.

"When I was in my first year at VMI—for any ignorant
people in the audience, that's Virginia Military Institute in
Lexington, Virginia—a brother rat bet me five dollars that
I wouldn't go to drill with no shoes on. I took him up on
it, feeling sure he wouldn't be able to come up with the five
dollars; but he scrounged quarters and half-dollars from his
friends, and sure enough, the bet was on!

"I had to put black shoe polish on my feet, even on the
nails and soles. I had to keep my toes close together, and
my feet as flat on the ground as I could. I was pretty
scared. Drilling at the Institute is serious business. That's
where Stonewall Jackson was a teacher, you know, and
where General George Marshall—"

"Yeah, we know," sang out Paul Chapin. "You've told us
before!"

"O.K. Anyway, I glanced down in the middle of the drill
and saw that the blacking had worn off the bottoms of my
feet. They were white as a babe's! But somehow, no officer
looked down that low, that day, and I got by, and collected
the bet. Five dollars was a lot of money in 1935!"

Bill is a good fellow, with a great wife, so we gave him a
big hand for his "mini-memory."

The next participant was announced by Chaplain Brewer, and Augusta Barton walked to the stage. I felt more than a little bit uneasy. Gusta's taste is not always the best.

"A woman in my home town," she began, "told her cook, Mamie, that she wanted the food at her dinner party to be extra good, and Mamie complied. The guests raved over the food, especially over the juicy apple pie with the unusual decoration on the top crust—little cuts in a pattern. One of the guests insisted on finding out how Mamie made the pie.

"So Mamie was called in and modestly gave her recipe.

" 'Well, ma'am, I jest cuts up the apples an' raisins an' nuts, an' puts 'em with some brown sugar and butter in the bottom crust. An' then I puts on the top crust, an' I takes out my top teeth, and I digs around in the crust with 'em, makin' a little pattern—' "

"Oh, Gusta! Stop it!" somebody yelled—a woman in the audience—bringing the selection to an abrupt halt. But the men thoroughly enjoyed the disgusting story.

There was a bit of confusion ensuing as Gusta—thoroughly enjoying the commotion—returned to her seat, and somebody called out, "Hattie McNair! Your turn!" I had planned to stay behind the scenes, so to speak, but pretty soon there was a chorus, so I had to get up.

I decided it was time for a poignant memory, remembering that Sidney's original idea had been for "reminiscences, both funny and poignant." So I told them one of my Alabama memories—the one about Grandpa's hat. They seemed to like it. After all, most of them have had brothers and all of them had grandfathers.

Cora Hunter was on next.

She said, "There was a girl in our small-town high school named Irma. I didn't know her very well. One afternoon my friend Helen and I were strolling through a meadow behind the school—talking about school and boys and church and boys and family and boys—and we met up with Irma, leading her family's cow home.

"Maybe she thought we were snooty. Maybe she didn't like our finding out that she had to tend to the cow. Anyway, without any warning she reached down and grabbed a part of the cow's equipment and sprayed us with milk from head to foot! I never did like milk much, in me or on me!"

We gave Cora a big hand for the good laugh she had given us. And I found myself thinking: *Dear Lord, please don't ever let the laughter stop. We need it, in this place.*

Lucius went up the steps to the stage next, shaking his head a little.

"I'm really reachin' back for this one!" he said. "I remember the very minute that I learned to whistle! I had been blowin' my breath through pursed-up lips for days— until my mouth hurt. I was six and my brother was eight, and he could whistle good, but all I could produce was wind with no sound.

"All of a sudden, when I was walking to school one day, I made a sound—a real note. I was Johnny-One-Note for a day or two, and then I finally graduated to 'Yankee Doodle.' Boy, was I proud!"

"I can go back further than that, Lucius!" called out Paul Chapin from the audience. He went up on the stage.

"I was about five when I learned to 'thump'—to snap my thumb and third finger together and make a popping sound—like this." He demonstrated. "I thought it was the greatest sound ever. I went around thumping for days, proud as punch. But I couldn't do it with my left hand. Still can't." He demonstrated his disability, and we clapped loudly, because we could all remember those long-ago triumphs and disappointments.

Paul left the stage, but Lucius stayed on. "What I told you about whistlin' was a real memory. Now I'm gonna tell you a taradiddle.

"I was drivin' across Charleston's Cooper River Bridge one day, and I saw a fellow poised on the edge of the bridge's highest point, gettin' ready to jump.

"'Don't jump!' I yelled, gettin' out of my car.

"'Why not?' asked the man. 'What have I got to live for?'

"'Think of your parents!'

"'No use. They're dead.'

"'Think of your wife and children!'

"'I'm not married.'

"By this time I was gettin' desperate. I scrambled around in my mind and yelled, 'Think of Robert E. Lee!'

"And you know what that dang fellow said: 'Who in the world is Robert E. Lee?'

"To which I replied, 'Jump, you Yankee!' And I got in my car. Didn't even look back!"

The crowd loved it.

Rose Hibben was next on the program. She has such a ladylike voice that we had to ask her to get closer to the microphone. (Nothing wrong with our ears, of course.)

Rose said, "The other day I asked a resident how she was feeling, and she said, 'Terrible! I'm as tired as if I'd been riding on a day coach all night!'

"That got me to thinking about train rides on the day coach, a long time ago. Cinders in your eyes and ears and hair, the old plush seats, grimy, the cars jerking just as you're about asleep. Babies crying, kids whining. Remember?"

There was much nodding of heads. She was surely taking me back.

"I remember a few good things about it," went on Rose. "One was the fellow—What did they call him? News butcher?—who would come through the cars with his wares. Remember those little glass telephones and lanterns he sold?"

Somebody in the audience called out, "Filled with teeny-weenie candy drops!"

"That's right," said Rose. "I loved them. Another good thing was lunchtime on a train trip. Mama used to fix enough food for a six-day march, and we were only going to Hamlet!

"The train had no sooner pulled out of our station at home when we'd start pestering her to open those shoe boxes. Hard boiled eggs, with salt in a little paper package; ham sandwiches; and fried chicken like they don't make any more. I can taste it now...and pickles—homemade pickles...and tea cakes.

"One thing we always had to do," she continued, "was check out the water cooler at the end of the car, about umpteen times. We even found the restroom fascinating...that teeny, tiny room. Why, I was coming down one day from North Carolina to Charleston on the Seaboard train, and a little girl about six years old went to the restroom. After a few minutes she began to bang on the door from the inside. Somehow the door had stuck.

"The child became panicky, of course, in that two-by-four-foot cage. She raised a ruckus. Her mother went to help, but she couldn't budge the door. Neither could the conductor or the brakeman. The conductor assured the mother, 'We'll get her out when we reach Dillon. They'll have the right tools there.'

"All the way to Dillon the child cried and yelled. 'Mama, am I *ever* going to get out of here?' she sobbed at one point. She had us all feeling upset and helpless.

"Well, of course they got the poor, exhausted girl out in Dillon by taking down the door. I've often thought of her, however, when I've been in a claustrophobic situation, wondering if I'm *ever* going to get out."

The people had enjoyed being reminded of childhood rides in day coaches, and had sympathized with the imprisoned child. They gave Rose an abundance of applause.

Now came the final storyteller of the evening, a quiet
man named Carl Royster. (I was really pleased that so many
men had been willing to participate.)

Carl said, "After I retired in 1980 I took up photography
and got real interested, not only in taking pictures, but also
in printing them. I took some of our old family photos and
restored them, making them clearer. People began paying
me to bring their old faded pictures back to life.

"One day a fellow from way out in the country came to
my house. 'Mr. Royster,' he said, 'I hear you're good with
old photographs. I've got one here of my granddaddy. I
liked the old guy, and I kinda hate to see his picture jest
fade away. Can you do somethin' with it?'

"'Well, Mr. Smathers,' I said, 'it's pretty far gone, but I
can try. That hat on his head—it's kind of beat-up, isn't it?'

"'Sure is,' he said. 'I don't suppose you could jest take it
off of him?'

"'I can try. It will take a little air-brush work. Tell me—
was his hair light or dark?'

"Smathers thought for a minute, and then said, 'Durn if I
can remember! But that's O.K. You'll find out what color it
was when you take his hat off.'"

We all had a good laugh over that story. We didn't know
Carl Royster had that much sense of humor.

The kitchen supplied light refreshments to end the
evening, and I heard lots of people saying they didn't know
when they had had such a good time. After the hall cleared,

Those dear, generous residents—bless their hearts!

the committee stayed behind to have the fun of counting the "take."

Christine and Louly lifted the bills in their hands and let them tumble back into the baskets.

"Money! I love money!" Chris said. "Aren't these bills beautiful? The ones are kind of tattered, but the tens are lovely!"

There were more tens than ones, thank goodness, and more twenties than tens! Those dear, generous residents— bless their hearts!

When we finished summing up, we felt overjoyed. "With all of this," I gloated, "added to what Sarah Moorer left for the Priest Fund in her will, we've got enough to buy them a new refrigerator! And that old gas range they have is pretty antiquated. I think I'll go to the appliance store tomorrow—"

"Now wait just a darn minute, Hattie," Lucius broke in. "You want us to start callin' you Miz Fullcharge? You talk like this is *your* money. How about lettin' that young couple have a chance to say what they need and want?"

I was properly taken down, and I apologized...Sam would have had a good laugh over that name: Mrs. Fullcharge. Am I that bad?...*Watch it, Hattie.*

We plan now to take the money—all of it—over to Arthur and Dollie on Sunday afternoon. I can hardly wait!

14

Welcome

March 29th

Dear Retta—

I haven't written to you in a long time, nor have I written in my journal in ages. I think I told you when you visited me that I'd been having painful tendinitis in my right hand, complicated by arthritis. It didn't get better, and finally a hand doctor (that's right—a bone specialist in Charleston now works only on hands!) had to operate, and is now treating me with cortisone and therapy.

I am gradually improving, thank goodness, because my left hand is a no-account appendage. I feel like slapping it sometimes when it won't tie or pick up or button anything properly. I'm surely not ambidextrous. In fact, I'm not sure I'm dexterous.

Anyway, I can type again, slowly, and am able to tell you that I'll be happy to welcome you here on May 1st! I didn't want to influence you, but I am delighted that you're coming to FairAcres. I'm convinced that you have the good sense to appreciate what's good here, and to ignore what's not. I think you've made a wise decision.

In your letter, I sense your apprehension. That's only natural. I know it's hard to give up the independence you now have, in your own home. I remember that my independence took on a great value when I made a move to give it up...I suppose it's a matter of independence versus security; and when no neighborhoods seem safe from vandals anymore, especially for lone women, security seems worth the sacrifice.

Companionship is a consideration, too. I found myself alone too much in my house. Here, at times, there's a surfeit of mortality, but you learn to deal with that; and there's always some nice person around to laugh with, or commiserate with; to play cards with, or watch an old movie with.

You're coming soon enough, too. That's *so* important. I've seen people enter this place in their late eighties, and the adjustment is much harder. Sometimes it never happens.

Our best news: Dollie Priest gave birth to a darling baby girl on February 2nd, and since I clued you in on the story when you were here, you will be glad to know that they've named her Louisa Canfield Priest! Louly is beside herself. She *beams*, and has made and embroidered a christening dress!

The baby will be baptized in our chapel next Sunday. Since we've practically adopted the little family, there will be a large turnout, I'm sure. Chaplain Brewer tells me he's having to brush up on the baptism service—He hasn't had much use for it in this place!

I should have told you, first, that Louly came into the dining room at lunch time one day in January, holding Arthur by the hand and holding up a small piece of paper: his driver's license! Everybody stood up and clapped, and Arthur hugged Louly, and there was sweetness and delight all over the place.

We heard yesterday that Arthur's wages have been increased considerably—For one thing, he can now drive The Home's vehicles. So maybe we'll be able to keep him for a while.

Now I suppose our next challenge will be to help him buy a secondhand car. Hurry up and get here! We need some new brains to pick for more money-making ideas.

See you *soon*.

Love from your old, *old* pal,
Hattie

P.S.: Tomorrow I plan to bundle up my journal—warts, typing errors, and all—and send it off to a publisher in Atlanta. I think I will call it "Out to Pasture," or maybe "The Poor Old Soul." Since I am completely unknown to any publishing house—and since I have no agent, the manuscript will no doubt make its way back to me pretty quickly. (I'll send a box with return postage.)

Who knows? Miracles *do* happen. Send up a little prayer for me, will you?

—H

About the Author

Effie Leland Wilder is eighty-eight years old, and *Out to Pasture* is her first novel. She has lived in Summerville, South Carolina, for fifty-eight years, eleven of them at the Presbyterian Home of Summerville, where she has served as president of the Resident's Council.

She graduated from Converse College in 1930 and received their Distinguished Alumna Award in 1982. She also received the Order of the Palmetto, the highest honor awarded from the state of South Carolina, in 1994. She has written feature articles for the *Charleston News and Courier*, had a short story published in *The Saturday Evening Post*, and co-authored *Pawley's Island: A Living Legend*.

The widow of Frank Page Wilder, she has three sons, a daughter, and seven grandchildren.

About the Illustrator

Laurie Allen Klein's artwork has appeared in *Atlanta Magazine* and *Athens Magazine*, and in her line of greeting cards. She has also volunteered her work for the Georgia Wildlife Federation. Klein works as a freelance illustrator and live in Madison, Georgia, with her husband and daughter.